BLOOD

— OF THE —

LILY

Also by S.D. Huston

Clash of Goddesses:
  Blood of the Lily
  Soul of a Rose (forthcoming 3 Jan 22)

Want to read the first three chapters of _Soul of Rose_? Sign up for my author newsletter at https://bit.ly/sdhuston-newsletter.

BLOOD
‑ OF THE ‑
LILY

S.D. HUSTON

Literary Dawn Press

BLOOD OF THE LILY

Copyright © 2021 by S.D. Huston

Contact Info: www.sdhuston.com
Cover Design by S.D. Huston
Edited by Faith Williams

ISBN: 978-1-7374298-0-7
First Edition: November 2021

DEDICATION

To my husband for his belief in me.
To Nissa Leder for pushing me.

PREFACE

Some of the stories and tales in this book are based on ancient narratives from various translations of the *Lebor Gabála Érenn* (*The Book of Invasions*) and the *Forbais Dromma Damgaire* (*The Siege of Knocklong*).

The *Lebor Gabála Érenn* has a variety of versions but it is a collection of poems and prose narratives in the Irish language intended to be a history of Ireland and the Irish from the creation of the world to the Middle Ages. Today it is regarded as myth rather than history. The *Forbais Dromma Damgaire* is a text about the legendary invasion of Munster by Cormac mac Airt.

This book is a work of fiction and some liberties have been taken with the translated texts such as providing motivations and reactions nonexistent in the original stories. Additionally, some place names used in this novel appear in Irish history or are known today, while others are completely fictious.

A glossary with approximate Irish pronunciations has been provided at the end of this book.

CHAPTER 1

"THAT'S A LEPRECHAUN!"

Lily raised a skeptical eyebrow at her sister Rose and her wild theory. Then she peered back through the interweaving branches of a blackthorn shrub. A leprechaun? No, just a very small man. But what was he doing in the middle of *An Caorthann Coill*, the Rowan Woods?

"It's because of Samhain." Rose's voice was barely above a whisper, but excitement laced each word. She bounced on her heels where she crouched among the lower branches of a fern tree. "The veil between worlds must be open."

A midmorning sun sifted through the canopy of rowanberry trees, highlighting the small man in the clearing. Probably no more than two or three feet in height, he hopped up and down, back and forth.

What was wrong with him?

The sun did little to dispel the gathering cold, which had strengthened over the last few days. A couple of leaves, still untouched by the season's cool breeze, tickled Lily's nose, and she swiped at her face before sneezing.

Samhain, huh. The celebration to welcome in the harvest and usher in the dark half of the year. Lily smirked. Some believed faeries existed and other nonsense, too. She blew blonde hair out of her eyes.

Once, it had been her favorite time of year, but that was before...

She shook her head. She didn't need the distraction.

"C'mon, Lil, you have to believe."

In what? The stories their mother often told them about the Otherworld? Lily waved a hand and rolled her eyes. Just stories. That's all they were, and now that they were both sixteen years old, they should have

1

grown past believing in such tales.

She knew from experience.

No good folk had saved Marigold, their other sister who had completed them as triplets. Now it was just the two of them.

Drawing in a breath and closing her eyes, she barely held back a grimace. When she opened them, Rose jutted her head toward the diminutive man, a crease deepening between her eyebrows.

His dark-red coat glinted, finely embroidered in more gold than Lily had ever seen in her life. He yanked his head back, showing his beard stuck fast in a fallen log. He muttered a string of curses as he pulled against the rough bark. His gray beard would have probably dragged on the ground, it was so long.

But what was the small man doing alone in the forest? For that matter, where did he come from? Lily heard of no one so small in any of the surrounding ráths or settlements.

These unanswered questions put her on guard. She didn't like strange things with no answers. Her hands tensed into balled fists.

Rose continued to vibrate with excitement, the emotion bright in her blue eyes. "Can you communicate with him?"

Really? He's a man. Not an animal.

"No, probably not," Rose said. "Even if he's a leprechaun, he's still not a land animal." She shrugged without looking at her. "We should help him."

Rose often forged ahead without thinking everything through. Lily placed a hand on her sister's arm, feeling the rough-spun sleeves of Rose's faded green dress where it peeked out from beneath her cloak. She wanted to say that she agreed, but the man, no matter how small, was still a stranger in their woods. And he was so close to their home, *Ráth Bláthanna*. They needed to be careful. When Rose peered back at her, Lily reached over her shoulder for a spear.

Rose sighed. "It would help if you'd talk once in a while."

Why? You understand me just fine.

Rose couldn't read Lily's mind, but as sisters who had shared the same womb, they understood each other well enough without words.

Pursing her lips, Rose unsheathed a dagger from her wide belt, moving between the thorny bush and fern, keeping the weapon at her side so as not to alarm the small man. Not being as discreet, Lily held the spear by the shaft, her lean body taut and ready for any adversary. The spear had been meant to catch food today, but that would have to wait.

She followed Rose closely, stepping into her sister's shoe impressions in the rain-soaked grass, until they broke into the clearing around the fallen tree. The man's curses grew louder as he hopped backward and forward like a dog tied to a rope, pulling on his beard at the same time.

"A thousand murders!"

Lily tightened her grip on the spear. Within the clearing, there was enough space to throw the weapon now. She tensed.

The struggling man saw them, and he stilled. Lines created deep grooves in his wizened face, like the ridges between mountains. He glared at them with fiery, red-rimmed eyes. "Why do you stand there? Can you not come here and help me?"

Rose moved forward and knelt next to him, studying how the beard tangled in the log. Meanwhile, Lily leveled her spear at the ready, but the small man dismissed her threat while he watched her sister tug on the wood. Nothing budged.

A gush of wind kicked at a pile of dried leaves and blew against them. Lily shivered. Rose tucked red curls behind her ears, her cheeks pinkening. "The tree hasn't started to decay yet." Sitting back on her feet, she still towered over the stranger. "What are you doing out here all alone, little man?"

"You stupid, prying goose!" He spat a wad of phlegm, barely missing Lily's feet. "I was going to split the tree to get some wood for cooking." He wiped his bulbous nose with an arm and pointed to the small ax on the ground beside him. "Thick logs burn the little bit of food I have. I need very little since I don't swallow so much as you greedy folk."

A sudden stricken look froze the man's face. His eyes swept back and forth, attempting to peer through the trees. He pursed his lips and whistled. "Here, boy!"

Lily looked over her shoulder, listening for any sounds beyond the natural environment. When the little man growled, she huffed. How was she to hunt with so much noise? He made enough racket to scare away all the creatures in a good dozen or more paces around them.

There goes dinner!

She couldn't make a mental connection with any of the land animals she'd ordinarily find in the woods, because they had gone too far away. There were limits to her ability.

"Dagda's balls!" He yanked on his beard, jamming the hairs deeper into the split wood. "I had just driven the wedge safely in, and everything was going as I wished, but the wretched wood was too smooth and suddenly sprang open. The tree closed so quickly I could not pull free in time, so now it's tight in."

Lily couldn't help smiling at the sight of the tree closing around the little man—the tree a predator and the man its prey. Imagine the dangers of being so small! It wasn't something she or Rose ever needed to worry about. They were as tall as most men, if not taller, at six feet high.

Rose chuckled aloud.

"Silly, milk-faced things! You laugh. Ugh! How repulsive you are!"

Rose straightened her back. "My apologies, stranger. But isn't there someone who could have helped you? Where are your people?"

"You senseless goose!" He snarled. "No people. You two are already too many for me. Can you not think of something better? Help me!"

Lily scowled and poked the man with her spear, just enough to leave a prick in his skin beneath the fine coat.

Foolish man. We should be hunting for our next meal instead of helping such an ungrateful stranger. So tired of tubers and beans. We should just leave him.

Rose hissed at her. "I know what you're thinking, but it's not right. He'd be defenseless in these woods. Wolves would surely find him and make a nice meal of him."

Lily pushed the spear tip a little harder.

"You flea-bitten fungus! You poked a hole in me."

At seeing a spot of blood dotting the man's shirt, Rose yanked Lily's spear out and shot her a glare.

Lily stumbled back a step.

To the stranger, her sister said, "I will help you." She brought her dagger forward, and in one quick motion, cut off the end of the beard.

Lily jolted with surprise at her sister's impulsive action.

"Uncouth girl!" The little man shook all over as he stepped away from Rose and the log, his gray beard in his two hands. It was still as long as his body, but it didn't touch the ground as it probably did before. He glared at them. "Curse these rude wretches, cutting off a piece of my splendid beard!" He growled, then he seized his ax and a leather bag that had been hidden among the roots of the tree and clinging ivy, swung it over his back, and scurried away.

Rose surged to her feet. "Wait, stranger!"

But the little man ignored her, advancing deeper into the woods without as much as looking at them again, muttering curses under his breath.

Rose cupped her hands around her mouth. "Are you a leprechaun?"

Tightening tree branches and shrubs quickly closed after the small-bodied man. Lily glanced at the piece of beard still stuck in the tree crevice. The gray strands seemed to shimmer when direct sunlight pierced the canopy overhead. She tilted her head, studying it, then dismissed it. She thought to head back to the main dirt path, but Rose seemed intent on the direction of the small man. Suddenly, a niggling sensation itched in the middle of her back, and she swung around.

Rose's eyes widened, suddenly alert as Lily scanned the forest.

No land animals had ventured forward still. She looked up. Perching upon a thick limb of an oak tree with bright-red leaves, an eagle openly perused her. His feathers were a dark brown all over except for a contrasting golden nape surprisingly visible at this distance.

Strange to see an eagle in such a cramped space.

As if the eagle had known what she was thinking, it so subtly dipped his head, dropping his large, strongly hooked bill. Just as Lily thought to tap Rose and direct her attention to the bird, he unfurled his long wings and dove straight at her with a piercing screech.

Lily ducked just as it swooped through the space above her. The eagle soared above the trees and disappeared.

CHAPTER 2

"MAY THERE BE A WIDOW'S CURSE on those shite girls!" Lugh fingered his shorn beard.

The forest continued an unsettled silence as he trudged through the tall grass and towering bushes, shouldering his bag of gold and precious gems.

He glanced up. Water beads hung suspended on the underneath side of pointed leaves. Something niggled at the back of his mind.

He saw himself as a giant, towering over most people.

He clicked his tongue. *When had that been true?*

Tucking his beard into the belt around his waist, he whistled. "Here, boy. Failinis!" *Where did that dog go?* He'd been missing for an hour.

Lugh scowled. *No, that couldn't be right.*

He didn't remember Failinis lying at his feet last night, so he had to have been gone longer. Lugh couldn't seem to now recall the day the hound had disappeared.

Well, he couldn't go home without his favorite dog.

Tilting his head, he listened for any sign. A familiar whine would have been enough, but nothing returned his call. He stomped his foot and slapped his leg.

A gurgling croak, rising in pitch, pierced the silence. Above him, a black raven stared at him. "What do you want, odious creature?"

Not waiting for an answer, he pushed through the tall grass. Wetness seeped through the cuffs of his long-sleeved jacket and soaked his trousers. A crack of thunder stunned him, and he froze. When the echo faded, he slowly turned around.

A beautiful young woman dressed in all black loomed over him. Her dress clung to her as a mist, sometimes solid; other times, parts faded, revealing white skin beneath. Her hair, as dark as a night without stars, fell along pale cheeks and rowanberry-colored lips. "Hallo, Lugh."

"Mórrígan." He grimaced. "What you here for?"

She tilted her head, her nearly black eyes piercing him where he stood. "You met the girls."

He lifted a shoulder, hefting his bag to the side.

When he didn't respond, she continued. "Which do you like?"

"Neither. Both are despicable."

"Don't be obtuse. We have a mission to accomplish."

With a hand, he pulled his gray beard forward. "The red-haired one cut my beautiful beard."

Mórrígan chuckled. "Still so vain, I see."

"You don't understand." He stomped his foot, heat suffusing his face. "My beard is the source of my power, and now I've lost Failinis."

"Your dog?" She slid her hands into the long sleeves of her midnight dress. The front dissipated in lazy swirls, revealing her full breasts before becoming opaque again. "That's not important right now. You need to choose one."

He stepped toward her. For a moment, he felt that she should fear him, even though she was at least twice his size. "Be gone with you."

A smile stretched her lips. "Don't forget, Lugh."

A thunderous roar sounded, and Mórrígan was gone, replaced by a raven that wheeled above the treetops and headed south.

He spit at the ground. The woman upset him every time he saw her. He couldn't remember why he loathed her, but then he didn't like most things.

As he turned back in his quest to find Failinis, he scrubbed a tear from his cheek.

CHAPTER 3

"GREAT GODS AND GODDESSES!" Rose sheathed her dagger. "I've never seen an eagle do that before."

Lily hadn't either. *What was going on today?*

She still looked after the bird's departure where, higher up, many branches were bare. The deluge of the past week's rain had stripped treetops. Trailing ivy hugged the bark of many trees. Another cold wind swept through the clearing, and she pulled the ends of her heavy wool cloak closer together. She trekked back to the dirt path. They needed to get the hunt on. With so many rainy days, their meat stores were depleted.

Maybe there was some truth to Rose's words. Two such extraordinary occurrences happening on Samhain seemed to support the assumption that the good folk could interfere in the natural world. *But was that really a leprechaun, or just a very, very small man?*

Rose followed this time, bounding to her side. A smile stretched the corners of her mouth wide. "Lil, we just saw a leprechaun."

She gave her sister a sidelong glance as she traveled the worn path. A leprechaun. A creature of myth and legend, one of the faery folk. For a moment, a little light burnt away the gray edges of misery that shrouded most of her waking moments. To believe in such magic. She shook her head, biting her lower lip.

Never forget.

This was the first Samhain without their sister, the sister who had completed them as triplets. An invisible weight threatened to drag her down. She laid a free hand over her heart, a stitch tightening there, and tried to take a deep breath. It stuck in her throat. Her nose tingled with a threat of tears.

She forced them back with quick blinking.

Rose caught her shoulders, forcing her to stop and face her. "Not again, sister." Her light, blue eyes moved over Lily's face, eyebrows lowered. "I miss her, too."

Lily released the air stuck in her throat and looked at the sweep of red hair flattened on Rose's forehead. A bead of water slipped down the strands. She flicked it away before slipping out of Rose's grasp.

"It wasn't your fault." Her sister's voice followed behind her. "I don't care what you believe. Her death was an accident. A senseless and tragic accident."

Lily jerked at each word. She opened her mouth to speak, but nothing came. She closed her mouth and shrugged.

"Gods, you're stubborn!" Rose huffed. "She wouldn't want you to waste your days in sorrow. Mourn her but move on."

How could Rose have let her sorrow for Marigold go so quickly? It had only been a few months since she died.

Lily looked back at her sister, who threw up her hands.

Just then, a twig snapped. Rose's eyes widened as her gaze focused over Lily's shoulder.

What else could happen today? Automatically, she sent out questing images to any nearby land animals, but they were silent. She peered into Rose's eyes. While Lily could communicate with land animals, her sister could communicate with sky animals, but Rose's head shake told her nothing.

Seeing that Rose still focused on something beyond Lily, she spun around, knuckles turning white on her spear shaft, and faced a new intruder.

A handsome, foreign man.

Tall, with skin darker than anyone she had ever seen, he held himself the same way warriors did, still but with an easy grace. His face was angular, and long, black lashes rimmed olive-shaped eyes. Dark hair curled around his face.

At seeing their defensive stances, he held up his hands. His richly embellished cloak swirled back, revealing a metal breastplate and a sheathed sword underneath. "Hallo."

His accent was heavy, not at all lyrical, as if he had just learned to speak their language.

Rose lowered her dagger. "What are you doing out here all alone, stranger?"

"I'm not alone." He looked over his shoulder before turning back to dazzle them with a smile, his teeth white in his dark face. "I heard voices, so I came to look while I was waiting."

Not alone? Were there others ready to ambush them?

Lily's entire body tensed, but his continued smile dulled her senses. His lips curved so nicely.

She squinted and cursed inwardly. No distractions. Ever so slowly, she inched into a better position to leverage her spear.

Rose returned his smile. "Waiting for what?"

"My guide." Deeply brown eyes shifted back and forth between them. "You might know her. *Bandraoi* Ana."

Rose clapped her hands and smiled.

Lily rolled her eyes at her sister but smiled as well. *Bandraoi* Ana was from the druidic order with a skill set in healing. However, she was also the love of their mother's life and as close to Lily and her sisters as a second mother. Before a time Lily could remember, Ana had made *Ráth Bláthanna* her permanent home and taught the girls how to use their *tíolacadh*, their gifts, for communicating with animals.

When Lily felt Rose relax, she jabbed an elbow into her side. Rose threw her a dirty look but took the hint. "What concerns do you have with Ana?"

"She told me that Lily and Rose could help me with a shortcut to *Oileán Dairbhre*."

Oileán Dairbhre, the Isle of Oaks, home to the *Ard-Draoi*, the High Druid Mug Ruith.

"Why would you need to go there?"

His smile slipped, the corners drooping. The inner corners of his eyebrows rose, but his eyelids loosened. And in the depths of his deep-brown eyes, something darkened.

Sadness.

Lily understood the emotion.

He ran a hand through his curls. "I'm looking for my brother, who is lost in this land."

Lily nodded. She knew about losing a sibling.

"Mug Ruith may be able to help me find him."

They knew the shortcut. It would be faster if they took him through the mountains instead of going along the coastline, where they'd have to stop at every *ráth* to make their presence known and avoid being attacked.

Rose shifted on her feet, her dagger lowering a bit. It was not in her nature to suspect others, so Lily nudged her again. Her sister's arm came back up. "Well, tell us now, stranger, who are you and what have you done with Ana? I don't see her anywhere."

With a boyish grin, he slapped an arm over his chest and tilted his head in a bow. "My apologies. My name is Quintus." Then he strode toward them, a brown hand extended.

Rose jerked, but Lily sniffed. What did he suppose we would do with that hand?

He shook his head, smiling again while lowering his arm. He stopped only a couple of paces from them. "I'm a Greek soldier."

So, this is what Greek people looked like. Although shipments of goods made it to *Ráth Bláthanna* a few times a year from the numerous states currently under Roman control, she had never seen one of the people until today.

"I'm Rose, and this be my sister, Lily." A pink blush spread across her cheeks as she introduced them.

Lily blinked at her sister. Did Rose fancy the man?

She pinched the bridge of her nose, but then caught the man studying her, his eyes intense. She tried to shrug off the feeling he stirred inside her. He was too nice-looking.

This close, his skin was like the color of algae swirled in mud. Golden flecks lightened his eyes. His cloak—a deep indigo color with yellow scrollwork on the edges—spoke of wealth, along with the manicured nails of the hand he dropped. However, calluses had lined the palm, evidence of his professed job. What did he do as a soldier?

Stirring lust tugged at her middle.

She lowered the butt of her spear to the ground with a loud thunk. What was she thinking? *He could be a slimy worm.*

Trying to recapture the Greek's attention, Rose bounced on her toes. "Where is Ana, then?"

Interestingly, a slight blush darkened his brown cheeks. "She had to take care of business."

"Business?"

Dark lashes lowered over his eyes. "Uh, personal business of a certain nature..."

"Oh!" Rose chuckled at his discomfort. "She should be back soon."

He nodded, probably relieved to not have to go into more detail.

Rose clapped her hands, excitement evident in her face. "Yay! You can stay with us tonight to celebrate Samhain. Then we can leave in the morning."

He nodded, his shoulders dropping a little. "I had hoped to leave sooner, but I understand."

Lily gazed over his body again. Going through the mountains was a rough trek. His thick cloak hid much, but she remembered the muscled forearm that had reached toward them a moment before. A very strong arm. Overall, good enough health and stamina to make the journey.

Again, her body reacted to her perusal of the Greek. Her cheeks heated. When did she become so foolish? Was it because there was a shortage of men her age? Better to concentrate on what mattered.

The hunt.

She touched Rose's arm in warning, then dropped to the ground, holding her spear upright, before closing her eyes.

Rose immediately understood, her voice barely breaking Lily's concentration. "We still need to find meat for tonight. Find the druidess, and we'll meet you back here."

Lily opened her awareness, reaching out around to test for the presence of wildlife. Although the small man had scared away most creatures, some had crept forward to forage again, deer and rabbits mingling together. They were near enough that she could communicate through vague images, but nothing concrete without a physical touch or closer proximity.

A single buck moved across her awareness. Careful, she touched upon his mind, hiding her intentions. She did not disguise her or her sister as friendly as she might have done had they only meant to pass through. She didn't like tricking the animals, but they needed this hunt. She was so tired of eating tubers and plants.

In a fluid motion, she leapt to her feet and plunged through the forest, the rain's clean scent mingling with the smell of dirt and wet leaves. Rose jogged next to her as the sound of *An Abhainn Bradán*, the Salmon River, gurgled nearby.

She kept her awareness open for any other dangers. They'd been ingrained since learning to walk to never to let their guard down while in the forests. Even with their gifts, attacks could come from wolves or reavers, mercenary soldiers who often scavenged for extra food, supplies, or whatever else they could steal from unwary travelers.

A bright light flickered in a tree ahead, almost giving her pause. As she came to the large rowanberry tree, nothing out of the ordinary appeared high up in its branches. Birds flitted from limb to limb, peering down on her and Rose. Her sister gestured ahead to her, communicating that the birds did not warn of any threats. Lily continued.

After a quarter of an hour, they came to a stand of tightly packed ferns and evergreens. She raised a hand and then slipped between them. The forest darkened as taller tree boughs interlaced above, blocking the sun. Winter's coming frost taunted each shadowed step.

In near silence, she came upon the buck, grazing alone in a cleared space between trees. As she balanced the spear in her throwing hand and faced the deer with her lead foot, she sent a prayer.

Flidais of the tangled wood, mistress of stag and doe and all free creatures, thank you for this wonderful gift. May this deer's body nourish our bodies, and may its memory nourish our souls.

Bringing the spear back, she rotated her hips slightly backward while keeping her lead foot firmly on the ground. Another twinkle of light out of the corner of her eye almost distracted her, but she ignored it, bringing her arm forward in a slight arch. She twisted her shoulder forward and pivoted on her back leg. The spear barely made a whistle as it sailed through the air and struck the buck squarely behind the shoulder.

CHAPTER 4

"THE CATTLE DISEASE HAS TAKEN much of the *taoiseach*'s stock."
Ana, one of the best druidic healers in *Clann Séaghdha*, glanced back at
Lily hauling the buck, the Greek man trailing behind her. The healer
walked next to Rose. Garbed in her usual earth-toned dress with a long
gray cloak, the healer almost blended into the surrounding forest with its
leafless deciduous trees.

Lily had always wondered why the *bandraoi* chose not to wear brighter
colors as most druids did to prove their high ranking.

Rose gasped with a hand to her mouth. "Oh no! What about the High
King's tribute?"

Lily frowned. Their own settlement only had five cows. What if the
taoiseach, their clan's chief, wanted to replace his diminished numbers to
give to the High King? They wouldn't be able to produce as much cheese,
their main trade with other settlements.

Ana shook her head. "The tribute's been paid, but next year could be
worse."

Lily took a deep breath, pulling on the makeshift litter of lashed tree
branches and ferns, the buck strapped on top. Noticing her more labored
breathing, Quintus offered to help, but she gave him a dark frown, cursing
his Greek blood. After countless hours spent in martial training and
extended periods of hunting, her body was toned and fit, but some days
had become harder since Marigold's death.

Sometimes she felt she had no strength left.

Ana stopped, forcing them all to pause, and Lily took the reprieve to
settle the litter to the ground. Even nearing middle age, Ana was a lovely
woman with deep-chestnut hair falling thickly to her waist and a tilted nose

that made her seem younger. Her eyes were a dark brown, like the evening shadows on the underside of a browning leaf. "Girls, you should know something I learned while at *Dún Neidín*." *Dún Neidín*, their chief's fortress settlement. "Rindal an Carragh has ordered you to marry."

Rindal the Scabby. Their *taoiseach*, the chief of *Clann Séaghdha*.

Lily closed her slack mouth and slapped a hand on one thigh. *May the banshee wail for his soul.*

Rose chewed on her thumb for several seconds, an action she often did while thinking. "So soon after Marigold...?" She couldn't complete the thought, but Lily understood.

How could the taoiseach *expect us to tie our fates to someone else's when we have had just lost our sister a few months ago?*

Ana turned to Rose and cupped her face in both hands. "I know, my love." She released Rose, then stepped to Lily to gather her callused hands in her own soft ones. "It has been commanded." When Lily pulled away from the *bandraoi*, her brows drawn, Ana gave her a small smile. Suddenly, Ana whipped toward the Greek. "Are you married, Quintus?"

The man spluttered for several moments. Then he wiped a hand over his face. "I am not, but my brother is all I care about at the moment."

With a faint smile and small shrug, Ana turned away and swept Rose forward with an arm, resuming their homeward journey. "Perhaps you will find more than your brother."

Quintus frowned.

After a quarter of an hour, they broke free of the tree line. A shout rose from the wooden palisade of their ráth. Most likely one of the Winkle brothers, so named for picking periwinkles one summer. He'd probably been made to stand watch while the others prepared for the celebration.

Lily held up a hand against a sun rising toward midday. Their circular *ráth* nestled in the side of a hill so large, it was almost a mountain. In spring, the hillside bloomed in dozens of colored blossoms, giving their *ráth*'s name of *Bláthanna*, or "flowers." But now, it was bare. Chill autumn winds blew over sweeping sections of dull green grass sprouting triumphantly through brown patches. In less than two months, winter would knock.

Lily grunted. *Be nice if one of the Winkle brothers came to help.* Her arms and legs ached. But this was her and her sister's lot because all the males of their homestead were either lame or too old or too young to hunt for the group.

Just then, Rose whooped in glee. The great wooden gate had cracked open, and a runner shot toward them.

As the tall young man drew nearer, Lily recognized his quick gait and wide smile. Not a Winkle brother. No, this was Failbhe, son of their aunt

Alannah, their mother's sister, and only two years younger than them at fourteen.

If he was here, that meant his family and a handful of warriors must be as well. His mother was married to the *taoiseach*'s son. Soldiers from *Dún Neidín* would have come to protect the chief's son and heir.

She scowled just thinking of the *taoiseach*. She didn't want to be forced into marriage, and not so soon after the loss of her sister.

That darkness threatened to weigh on her again, and she reveled in it for a moment. Sadness churned beneath her breast. Sometimes she wondered if she liked to feel sad, finding herself there so often.

Marigold would have danced in front of them, twirling around, looking for any flowers leftover from the storm. These she would have woven into their hair or slid behind their ears, laughter following each step she took. She had the widest smile.

Lily yearned for her lost sister.

When Failbhe stopped in front of them, he rested on his spear, barely winded. "I see you, Líle níc Muaich. I see you, Rós níc Muaich. I see you, *Bandraoi* Ana." His eyes slid curiously over the Greek man.

Lily nodded, but Rose laughed out loud, an arm across her belly as she bent forward. Lily raised an eyebrow at her, but Failbhe chuckled. Somehow, his attempt at solemnity amused them both, but Lily didn't understand it. Settlements lived and thrived by virtue of being wary and vigilant.

When their cousin softly bumped a palm on Rose's arm, her sister straightened and wiped a tear from her eye. She threw back her shoulders and tried a serious voice in her response. "We see you, Failbhe mac Diarmuid Mór, and may I introduce Quintus the Greek."

Trying to match Rose's seriousness, Failbhe nodded to the Greek.

Chewing her thumb again, Rose attempted to hold back another laugh, the fit finally busting through her mouth as she failed. She threw an arm around the youth's neck to pull him close and tilted her head against his. "You've grown another head taller."

A light warmed his face at Rose's observation. "I'll be as tall as both of you one day."

Lily clicked her tongue at the reminder of their unusual height for women. They both towered over Ana. But Rose pushed off his shoulder with a chuckle. "Next summer." Her smile made her beautiful. "Look at you. Already a warrior, if I do say so myself."

Failbhe beamed. He was finally the age to be considered a full-fledged soldier and protector for his people.

Rose gestured behind her at the litter. "All right, warrior, take the load for Lily." She laughed again as he groaned, but he took the burden, allowing them to continue unencumbered as they trudged the rest of the way uphill to the walls of their *ráth*. "Wait until you hear what we found in the forest before meeting up with Ana." When their cousin opened his mouth, Rose shook her head. "I will tell the story for all to hear."

Failbhe moved a little faster.

Voices and music grew louder as they neared the wooden walls. The smell of wood-burning fires and sizzling meat wafted to greet them as the gate groaned open to welcome them home.

Saliva pooled in Lily's mouth. It had been several days since they had meat, and today, it seemed she would have her fill—not only the buck but someone had brought a pig for the roast. She may love land animals with her innate ability to communicate with them, but she loved them almost as much for the nourishment they provided.

With a wave to Odhran the sentry, the older of the Winkle brothers at eleven years of age, they swept through the causeway and inside to a whirlwind of activity, a difference from the sleeping settlement they had left in the early hours of the morning.

The circular homestead had come alive with song, women's gossip, men drinking, and children chasing each other and laughing. The central fire in the *lis*, the courtyard, blazed brightly. Another pit had been dug to light a fire under the roasting pig. Everyone anticipated the evening's feast.

Their small settlement housed a dozen people at any given time, but here there had to be close to fifty or sixty filling the *lis* now. *Where would they all sleep?* The *ráth* boasted of only three roundhouses.

On the ground, most likely. Close to warm fires and wrapped deep in fur blankets.

Lily recognized most of the visitors and families from surrounding homesteads, but others were unknown. One unfamiliar old man perched on a great log pulled close to the central fire. He crouched over a wooden staff, napping and nonthreatening enough.

However, other strangers raised the hair on her arms. A group of foreign warriors kept a close circle around a purple-caped visitor. Lily uselessly stretched her neck for any clue to this stranger but settled on perusing the soldiers.

Although their heavy wool cloaks of either gray or faded yellow followed local customs, a curious piece of long fabric wrapped around their necks. She guessed that it helped them keep warm, but it seemed less useful bunched under the chin. These warriors didn't appear to be from her homeland, especially since they had a darker skin tone like Quintus.

Were they Greek, too?

"No, it's true. Tell him, Lil."

During her study, Lily hadn't heard whatever tale her sister had spun.

But a group of curious faces had clustered around them, while others leaned forward from their seats at the nearby central fire. Rose seemed to notice her inattention and frowned. "Tell them about the leprechaun we saw in the forest."

"Leprechaun?" Quintus had followed them even though Ana had left their sides. The deer was already being hung up to bleed out.

Biting the inside of her cheek, Lily demurred. A deep laugh filled the void. With legs stretched to the fire, *Dún Neidín*'s head warrior, Máel Maud, quieted his laughter after a few more guffaws. "A leprechaun! You're daft, girl."

Somewhere among the gaggle of listeners, one of the men called out. "What stories you do tell, Sneachta Bán and Rós Dearg!"

Snow White and Rose Red.

The men laughed even louder and harder, pounding a knee or each other on the back.

Lily crossed her arms at the names. Supposedly, they were two heroines in a story from some far east land. She'd heard it once. Two naïve sisters who went everywhere together and ended up marrying two prince brothers. The story had been too sweet.

But the story was also a reference to their hair color, Rose with her red curls and her with her blonde hair so faint in hue it nearly matched an old woman's color. Whenever it had been just her and Rose, this was the nickname the men had given them. When Marigold had been alive, the three of them together had been known as *Na Cailíní Bláth*, the flower girls. Once, Rose had asked their mother why she had given flower names to them, something so untraditional for their land of Éire.

The answer had been a strange one. "Your mother loves flowers."

Ciara, their mother, had never offered any other clarification.

Rose took a step forward, her chin inching up. "I'm telling the truth."

Her declaration and the men's laughter sparked interest from the surrounding clusters of people. A hush fell over the crowd; only the echoes of some dogs fighting over a bone filled the circular enclosure.

Rose held out a palm to Lily, her sister's eyes imploring her. "I swear on our father's grave. Say something, Lil."

She chewed her lip for a moment as multiple heads swiveled to look at her. Words failed to come to her lips. She hadn't always been mute. It was just easier after...

After Marigold died. It made people stop asking her whether she was okay or tell her that the pain would lessen one day.

She could speak. She just didn't want to. Besides, not speaking reminded her that she hadn't been able to save her sister, and her voice had become hoarse since that day she had yelled Marigold's name over and over while plowing through the ocean, salty water filling her throat and lungs.

She sighed. She also couldn't fully agree with Rose's fanciful thinking, even if they had gifts. She lifted a shoulder, then held a hand close to the ground.

"Teeny, tiny!" Dramatically swinging one arm over the other, Rose hovered her hands closer together, exaggerating the stranger's small height, her neck stretched forward. "No way a real man could be this small. He had to be a leprechaun."

Voices clamored over one another as they bombarded Rose and Lily with questions. Lily tried to shrink into the ground. What she wouldn't give to be the small man's height now. Ever so slowly, she slipped away from the group. Even Quintus was enthralled by the conversation. It helped that Rose was the more dramatic one.

Once free, Lily heaved a sigh.

She headed to a roundhouse set back off the main path to the right, the home she shared with their mother and Ana, her elderly grandmother, Rose... and Marigold. Why did it feel like all she had to do was enter the warmth of their home and she could still find Marigold? Marigold smiling her secret smile while sweeping back her riot of golden curls. Her ghost lingered in the shadows, her scent on her blankets, her laughter caught in the timber frame.

This time last year, Marigold and Lily had pranked the Winkle brothers by building a life-sized doll out of straw and setting it up in the field outside the main gate. Marigold had called it a scarecrow, something she learned about from one of the neighboring homesteads, but it had frightened the young boys so much that they wouldn't leave the walls of the *ráth* until Marigold and Lily took it back down, laughing the whole time.

A pang shot through Lily's chest, and she placed a hand over it, dipping her head. She closed her eyes, her feet slowing. She missed the special bond she'd had with her sister. Marigold had been the oldest, having been born first of the triplets, with Lily being the youngest.

Behind closed eyes, sounds became sharper. Children laughed. A cow lulled. Subtler noises buzzed, that of clucking chickens and juices sizzling as it rolled off the roasted pig's tightly stretched skin, falling into the fire.

She reopened her eyes in time to side-step half a dozen children playing a game of chase. As she neared the group of strange warriors who stood between her and her family's roundhouse, she clenched her fingers a little tighter around her spear's shaft. A couple of them took notice of her, their dark-colored, olive-shaped eyes assessing her. The younger of the two rose black eyebrows and the corner of his lips turned up. When she didn't return the smile, he scowled and dismissed her. The other warrior had already trained his eyes past her, finding little threat in her appearance.

Something tingled along her skin, and because she kept an eye on the two warriors, she barely caught herself from falling when a dog leapt in front of her. She jumped with a small yelp, and the animal stilled, his brown eyes moving across her face.

She didn't know this greyhound, and he didn't know her, but never had she seen such a beautiful dog or one that stood so tall, his back nearly as high as her hips. She knelt in front of him in awe, her head coming just to his chest. His sleek fur was parti-colored, and it shone under the weak fall sun. She lifted a hand, palm up, and stretched her mind toward his.

This close she could speak, and he would understand her. But she hadn't said a word in so long, she wasn't sure what her voice would sound like.

Instead, she made a connection with him through touch, the strongest connection she could have with any land animal.

Images flooded into her awareness, one after the other, and they came so quick that she couldn't make sense of them. Only one thing kept coming back. A brilliant, golden light. She bit her cheek, unsure of what to make of the dog's communication, but his love for his owner came through in that golden light, whoever he or she was. When Lily echoed images back to him, creating pictures of her family for him, he barked and licked her face, almost knocking her over with his exuberance.

The dog breath heated her chaffed cheek, and she chuckled as she pet him.

"Jason!"

Lily glanced up and was again astounded by the beauty before her. This was the purple-caped stranger from earlier who now stood over her. The strange woman was the most alluring living being Lily had ever encountered. Her radiance seemed to shine from her very skin. Beneath the cloak's hood, a golden band circled her forehead, holding back dark hair from a graceful face. Delicate gold spirals swung from her ears.

Kneeling on the ground still, Lily spoke before she noticed the words coming out of her mouth, and they came out breathless and hoarse. It had been months since she had spoken. "You're beautiful."

The woman blinked at her.

Embarrassed, Lily stood and wiped down the front of her man's tunic before pulling the ends of her drab wool cloak together. Her own rough clothing reminded her that the woman's finer clothing and jewelry signified a high rank. The golden band meant she was royalty from somewhere.

The dog whimpered and nudged Lily's hand.

The woman looked down at the dog, her hood shifting enough to reveal a single peacock feather pinned to the side of her head. "There you are, Jason. Come."

Jason? What kind of name was that for a dog?

Lily pat Jason one last time, before withdrawing her hand. Two warriors flanked the woman, and Lily mentally kicked herself. She should have been more aware, but the woman's appearance had distracted her.

"Curious. Jason hasn't let anyone touch him but me." The woman looked her over. "What's your name, girl?" Even if the strange woman hadn't been wearing such expensive clothes, her demanding tone made it clear she was used to getting her way.

But then, even if Lily hadn't wanted to respond to such arrogance, she spoke as if compelled. In the same breathless tone, she said, "Lily, like the flower."

The woman hummed for a moment. A slight smile played on her lips. "My favorite flower." Her small, gloved hand darted out and grasped a few strands of Lily's white-blonde hair. "You think I'm beautiful?"

Not able to speak this time, Lily only nodded and gulped hard.

The woman released her hair. "We used to thrive on such adoration."

Lily crinkled her forehead. *What did that mean?*

With her chin raised, the woman maintained a regal bearing as she turned slightly to the soldier on her left. She whispered a few words and the man placed something in her gloved hand. Then she squared back on Lily. "Give me your hand, Lily like the flower."

She complied, and the woman placed a gold coin into her palm, the metal cold against her skin.

"That is my mark. Should you ever need help, you only need to call." Without further thought for Lily, she moved away from her.

Lily snapped her mouth shut and looked down at her pale hand, palm still up. The gold coin with a woman's likeness gleamed. Never had she held this much gold. In fact, she couldn't remember the last time she'd held any gold. Coins weren't used anywhere on the peninsula, but gold was valuable. She wondered if it could be melted down. Perhaps have a piece of jewelry made of it.

Not much she could do with it now. She slipped it into a pocket she had sewn into the folds of her tunic below the belt. Finding a stronger voice after a quick cough, Lily was finally able to project herself. "Who are you?"

The woman glided to a stop and looked over her shoulder. The smile on her face seemed to contain secrets that Lily would never know.

"Hera."

CHAPTER 5

"WOULDN'T YOU CONSIDER marrying me?"

From her rest against a log pulled to the central fire, Lily smirked up at Dermot, a cousin through marriage. Golden-brown curls crowned his youthful face. With long, graceful fingers, he strummed a musical chord on a harp and sang a few lines. Even though he was a year younger than her, his voice was deep, except when he sang. His falsetto tone belied his gruff speech, characterized by a breathy and flute-like sound.

She'd always liked his voice, and it had paired well with Marigold's when they had joined together in song.

There were no blood ties between her and Dermot because he was related to the *taoiseach* from the other side of the chief's family. He had come with Failbhe and his family because he was the only unmarried and unrelated male in all the surrounding *ráth* and settlements. When they were younger, the talk was that Dermot would marry one of *Na Cailíní Bláth*, the flower girls, to solidify clan ties. It made sense that she would be his choice because she shared a love for playing the harp. In fact, after he'd received training on the harp himself, he'd taught her everything he knew.

Unfortunately, her feelings had always been nothing more than love for a brother. But, if the *taoiseach*, the chief and leader of *Clann Séaghdha*, had commanded Dermot to marry either Rose or her, then what choice did she have? She clenched her jaw.

He held his harp out to her. "Care to play a tune?"

She took the instrument, relishing the smooth oak in her hands, and her body relaxed. Her fingers played over the strings. Sadness slipped in as she thought of Marigold, her shoulders drooping forward. Many evenings

Lily would play the harp and Marigold would sing in her angelic voice, Rose dancing around the pair of them.

She reveled in those memories, hoping they never faded, and a tune began in her head, a song of her own forming. In a low voice, she sang while playing the chords. *"Soft winds sighed across the sea the day we played in clear waters. Then a wave bent your knee..."*

Her fingers stilled when tears clouded her eyes. She couldn't complete the song, so she shook her head and handed the harp back.

Dermot took it but placed a hand on her shoulder. "Oh, cousin." He cupped the back of her head, running his fingers through her fine hair. "Music can heal if you let it."

Feeling a loss from giving the harp back, she bit her lip. Tears threatened to spill over her bottom lashes. She hunched her shoulders forward, shutting out Dermot. She didn't want to share anything with him. It was too painful.

So, he withdrew his hand.

"All right, now is not the time, but I had hoped to talk." When she didn't look at him, he continued. "We've always had a close bond, so... I want to say..." He cleared his throat. "I mean to put forward that you should choose me as your husband."

His feelings had to be beyond brotherly. She grimaced.

Lily wasn't sure Dermot saw her reaction, but he pressed on in her silence. "Please consider it. I would be honored to pair with you."

She shrugged and drew her knees to her chest. She felt him move away when she refused to respond, and she released a stuttered breath, grateful to be alone.

What was the boy thinking?

She didn't deserve happiness or to take someone else's. It was her fault Marigold was gone forever, and it hurt worse that today was a day they both favored more than others.

She closed her eyes, exhausted mentally and emotionally. Tears pricked hot against her eyelids. The weight of her sister's death constantly reminded her that she didn't deserve to outlive Marigold, and now she had to marry someone. Someone she would make absolutely miserable.

Heat licked her face, and soon it was so warm that she unclasped the brooch holding her cloak together in the front and pushed the material back, where it caught on the leather harness for her spear.

Conversations and laughter still hummed in the air, but everything was muted in her misery. It was as if she existed outside the space and time of that moment, and it reminded her how lonely she was. Times like these broke her self-control. She let the tears flow.

Whenever she thought about a future where the tears would stop, guilt tripped her. She couldn't allow herself to let go, because if she did, that meant she'd have to let Marigold go. She didn't want to lose the memories of her.

Afraid to forget her. Afraid she'd make the same mistake again, and she couldn't—wouldn't be responsible for letting anyone else die.

"Lily."

Her mother's voice halted her tears, and she opened her eyes. Ciara stood over her, Rose and Quintus a pace behind. Her mamaí knelt next to her and rubbed the back of her small hand across Lily's wet cheeks. The corners of her eyes tightened.

"My poor girl," she whispered. Compared to Rose and the Greek soldier, Ciara was diminutive, at barely five feet tall. "Come, daughter."

Dutifully, Lily stood, drawing her cloak back over her shoulders against the cold, clasping it together over her breasts, and then grasped her spear, which she had lain on the ground nearby.

Although short, Ciara's stride was long and quick as she navigated their way out of the *ráth*, down the hill, and back into the forest, leaving behind the curious eyes of their visitors. They followed the worn trail, the afternoon sun chasing away the worst of the cold. Laughter and conversation muted in the wall of trees.

Ciara didn't stop until they came to *An Abhainn Bradán*, the Salmon River. Here, she picked up a few rocks and skipped them over the water. "I could not say this where anyone would possibly overhear. Not with so many of the chief's men nearby." She took a deep breath. "I know what the *taoiseach* has said, but you will not marry."

Lily furrowed her brow, but Rose spoke for them both. "What? If we don't obey, we'll be banished."

Ciara set her mouth in a grim line. "You are not to marry." She skipped a last rock, then turned to grab each of their hands, her small fingers weaving with theirs. "The good folk have another plan."

Rose placed her free hand on her chest, a crease between her eyes.

Lily chewed the corner of her lip. *Mamaí had to be crazy. The good folk were not real.*

The Greek cleared his throat. "I guess this is where I come in."

Ciara smiled, the tightness around her eyes loosening. "My prayers to the Great Mother Goddess have been answered. Continue with your plan to escort Quintus to Mug Ruith but ask the *Ard-Draoi* about your future."

The Greek took a step closer to the river, looking at how it flowed downward, away from *Ráth Bláthanna* in the distance. "Perhaps you could help me find my brother instead of returning."

Ciara nodded, looking out of the corner of her eye with doubt. "That is one possibility."

"But what about you, Mamaí?" Rose asked.

"This is about your futures." She released their hands and sighed. "Remember my favorite story?"

Their mother loved to tell stories about the Tuatha Dé Danann, a race of supernatural people who had settled the land centuries before them. Like Lily and her sisters, the ancient peoples also had gifts.

Lily glanced at the Greek, who looked confused, but Rose nodded. Quintus inched nearer, almost brushing against Lily so that she smelled a faint musk scent from his indigo cloak. It reminded her of the forest.

Ciara cleared her throat. "Niamh Chinn Óir, Niamh of the Golden Hair, was a faery queen of *Tír na nÓg*. But she was very lonely. You see, her father, the son of the sea, Manannán mac Lir, had built her a beautiful castle, but she had no one to share it with, and she longed to have children."

A bright smile split Quintus's face. "Was Poseidon Manannán's father?"

"Poseidon?" Rose jerked an eyebrow up. "No, Lir is his father. Mac means son of, so that Manannán mac Lir means Manannán, son of Lir."

Scratching at dark stubble on his chin, he shrugged.

Ciara continued the story after the brief interruption.

"Niamh had watched our lands for many years, when she finally found a man who made her heart stop. This man was Oisín, son of Fionn mac Cumhaill. Not only was he handsome, but he was a skilled warrior, a poet, and a bard. She vowed to love him forever.

"Riding her white horse, Enbarr, across the seas, she passed through the fog, leaving her homeland for his. When she found him, she told him of her wonderful land, where no one ages or is ill, where there is no hunger or war, the weather is always warm, flowers always bloom, and everyone is happy. She asked him to live with her in *Tír na nÓg*, the Land of Youth, a realm of the Otherworld."

Ciara always liked to pause here for dramatic effect, but Quintus took advantage of the silence. "Mortals can live with the gods?"

Lily shook her head at his ignorance. She knew about the Greek gods and goddesses, so why didn't he understand Éire's deities?

Rose was the one to answer him. "The gods do not sanctify a place against mortals. If you can find a way there, you're able to stay."

"No mortals are allowed on Mount Olympus." He ran a hand through his hair. "Your gods are still powerful, right? Like the one who can control the sea."

Rose put her hands on her hips. "Which one? Both Manannán and his father, Lir, are gods associated with the sea."

Quintus scrubbed a hand on the back of his neck. "Sounds confusing to me. My gods are pretty straightforward. One controls the sea, another the sky, and the other the underworld."

Ciara clicked her tongue at their interruptions, drawing their sheepish glances back to her story. "At first, Oisín was undecided. He didn't want to leave his father, or the Fianna, his father's warrior band. Niamh feared he would not choose her even though he found her attractive, and she was afraid to be alone for the rest of her life, so that night, she snuck into his tent and seduced him.

"The next morning, she told him that he was free of her, because she would always have a part of him. She laid a hand on her belly, and he knew that she carried his child. Oisín felt he'd been tricked, but he would not abandon his child, so he agreed to live with her in *Tír na nÓg*. Although the union is not always a happy one, they became parents to two sons and a daughter: Oscar, Fionn, and Plor."

Ciara eyed each of her daughters. "But that is not the end of the story."

Something caught Lily's eye beyond her mother, farther down the bank of *An Abhainn Bradán*. She brought her spear up ever so slightly.

"Their children also wanted to find love and happiness..."

Lily stepped around her mother, Ciara's tale trailing off again as Lily scanned the riverbanks.

There!

Something like a giant grasshopper bounced by the water.

Lily sprinted forward, her mother calling after her. Rose reacted just as quickly, running to catch her, then past her. No one could beat Rose in a foot race.

As they neared the spot, they found it wasn't a grasshopper. No, this was the same miniature man in his red coat and shiny buttons.

Together, she and Rose edged a few steps in his direction, trying not to startle him, but then he jumped toward the water as if to leap in, and Rose vaulted forward.

"What are you doing?" Rose's voice echoed. "Surely you don't want to go into the water? You'd freeze before swimming two paces."

"I am no such fool!"

It was then that Lily saw the little man's beard tangled in a fishing line from a pole he'd fashioned for himself, and it seemed a big fish had taken his bait. However, the unamiable little fellow didn't have enough strength to pull it out, so now the fish twisted about, pulling him closer and closer to the water's edge.

Rose bent down to work on the line. In a moment, Lily was by her side, helping her while the man held on to all the reeds and rushes nearby. Little good that did him, because each time the fish yanked around, he was forced to follow the movements.

"That accursed fish wants to pull me in." He jumped back when a little slack came to the line, but the movement pulled the line from the girls' hands.

Lily reached for him, holding him fast, while Rose worked on his beard.

Quintus's voice came to her from above, where he stood over her. "What a small man."

"It's no use." Rose dropped the line and reached for the knife on her hip. "It's all tangled fast together." There was nothing to do but to cut the beard again, making it a clean break.

The small man screamed as the knife slid through his beard. "Is that civil, you toadstool, to disfigure a man's face? Was it not enough to clip off the end of my beard? Now you have cut off the best part of it, completely spoiling it. I wish you had been made to run the leather off your shoes."

With that, he plucked a sack out of the rushes, and without another word, he dragged it with him as he jumped into the water. A small plop echoed. Then he was gone.

Lily's mouth gaped open. She couldn't understand why they had saved the man from the water if he just meant to jump in all along. She searched the riverbank anyway, her stomach flipping at the sight and hoping he didn't drown. How could he possibly survive such cold waters?

Quintus stood next to Rose now, Ciara but a pace behind them. The Greek soldier looked dumbfounded.

"That was the smallest man I've ever seen." He wiped a hand over his face. "How does he survive? For that matter, how does he..." He glanced at Ciara and cleared his throat. "How does he properly love a woman?"

Lily grunted as she gave up her search.

Ciara led them away from the river until they found the worn path leading back to their *ráth*.

Quintus continued with his amazement. "He's so small that he'd be lost in a woman's bosom for days."

Ciara frowned back at him, and he closed his mouth.

Lily smiled. She and Rose might still be innocent in the ways between men and women, but they'd been around enough fornication, human and animal alike, to understand the basics.

Then, once again, something caught her eye. A shiny flickering light, not unlike the one she'd seen earlier that day in a tree. The others were oblivious to the twinkling, jabbering on still about the small man, which Rose named as the leprechaun.

The Greek's deep voice floated back to Lily. "If that was the leprechaun, where's his pot of gold?"

Lily rolled her eyes at his question, then moved toward the shadows, where trees and shrubs closed in tightly together, peering into the darkness. It was in this murkiness that the light glimmered again.

She charged into the dense brush.

"Lil!"

Rose couldn't slow her down, because when that light flared, she saw Marigold.

She scrambled through the tightly woven arms of bushes, ferns, and low trees, nearly fumbling over an exposed root. When given space to run, she took off after the light. It moved further into the great forest. Lily was sure it was her sister with her golden curls. She ran as fast as she could.

At first it didn't matter how much ground she gained, barreling through bushes and scraping and banging up her body to reach the light, because she didn't get any closer or farther away.

Then, she was on it suddenly as she broke through a pair of evergreens.

She stopped as the light wavered in front of her.

It was Marigold.

Resplendent in a white gown she had never owned and outlined with a golden light, her sister smiled at her. She looked nearly the same as she did before she had drowned in the ocean. Her blue eyes so light, her curls of burnished gold cascading over her shoulders.

Marigold opened her mouth to say something, then she vanished.

The forest darkened all around Lily, and she stood there, too stunned to move. Her heart beat in her ears. Sweat pooled in her palms.

Faint sunlight broke free to stream through the tree boughs above. A rustle nearby turned out to be the silhouette of a deer, a fawn behind her, and Lily felt the doe's life-force, her intentions. The deer acknowledged her with an image of the forest, familiar with Lily and seeing her as part of the natural surroundings. She bent her graceful neck to nibble the few struggling shards of green grass, moving over for her fawn.

Still, Lily didn't move.

Had Marigold really stood in front of her, or had it been her ghost? Maybe it had been a delusion.

Whatever it was had disappeared.

She scrubbed two tears trekking down her cheek. She had just seen her dead sister, but now Marigold was just as lost to Lily as before.

She fisted her hands against her thighs and yelled.

The doe and fawn leapt away.

Her roar had been a guttural sound. One of frustration and longing.

Defeat ballooned in her chest, and she slapped a hand over it, gritting her teeth.

A high-pitched whistle sounded above her, and through a wash of tears, she saw an eagle sitting in a tree, outlined in a stream of light. She tilted her head while wiping away her tears, and curiously, the creature also tilted his head, showing his golden nape. It was the same eagle from before.

He chirped.

She furrowed her brow. She didn't have time for the silly creature. "Whist."

Finding her entry point between the evergreens, she weaved between the silent trees. After several moments, doubt niggled her mind. She searched for clues of her passage—broken twigs, flattened grass—but her tracks were harder to see the farther she traveled into darkened areas. After several minutes, she was sure she was lost. She peered up to get a sense of the sun's position, but too many tree boughs blocked the sun's location.

She paused in her hike and took a deep breath. How else could she find her way? It shouldn't be too hard. She'd spent plenty of time in the *An Caorthann Coill* with her sisters, exploring the woods, losing themselves only to challenge themselves to find their way back.

Deep breaths softened the heartbeat in her ears. She closed her eyes. Leaves rustled. A twig snapped. A whoosh of wings beat the air.

The sound of those wings neared, and her eyes popped open in time for her to duck. The eagle had followed her. Surely he found it difficult to fly in such close quarters, but still he hovered near her, flapping his wings, the tips brushing the lowest tree limbs. He struggled to stay afloat, flying up, then down. Then he swooped at her, and she straightened and ran.

She scrambled through heavy foliage again. Something snatched her hair, the strands ripping free, but she didn't stop. After several minutes, her side clenched, and she found a spot beneath a low outcropping of rocks. She slid into the small space, breathing heavily.

Crazy bird!

Just as she closed her eyes to listen to the forest again, she heard Rose call her name.

CHAPTER 6

As THE SUN GRACED the eastern mountaintops, bright red splashed across the sky, overtaking the more calming pastel colors fringing wispy clouds. Winter's warning came in a burst of wind. Lily ushered *Ráth Bláthanna*'s few sheep and cows through the gates of the wooden palisade, looking over her shoulder with a worried frown. As she completed her chores, she continued to search the brown plains rolling downward to the edge of the forest.

She saw no sign of the Greek man, whom they lost in the woods hours ago.

A single lamb followed her every step, keeping Lily's mind filled with a steady stream of images. The tumble of pictures told her the lamb had missed her this day, even though she had only been derelict in her duties to the animal for a few hours. This warmed her heart more than anything else had recently, except maybe seeing her sister's ghost. She wanted to slide all the way into the cozy feeling. Escape her sadness.

But that wasn't realistic. Neither was thinking that Marigold had actually come to her. To reassure the lamb and herself, she scratched the animal behind the ears.

She had to stop letting Rose's fanciful thinking about Samhain affect her thoughts.

By the time she was done bringing in all the livestock and checking their food and water supplies, darkness laid a mantle on the sky. She helped Rose close the gates for the night, securing everyone inside from the dangers of night animals and roving reaver bands.

Samhain festivities continued within the *ráth* with rounds of ale, good food, and throngs of singing and dancing. Firelight etched shadows all around.

Rose bounced on her toes, ready to join the dancing, but Lily wanted to sit with her thoughts, reflecting on the lost Greek man. She shook her hands, her fingers aching as the air cooled quickly without the sun. She longed for the solitude of her family's roundhouse even as Rose dismissed any concerns beyond a quick dance and warm ale.

Lily just wasn't in the mood for celebration. She leaned a hand against the cold gate and bent her head to the wood, closing her eyes, wishing the Greek would reappear.

Rose placed a hand on her shoulder. "I don't like it either."

Lily looked at her sister, knowing her face reflected the haunting feeling in her soul. Her misty breath suspended as an eerie ghost between them.

What if he froze to death?

Lily hunched her shoulders forward, pushed away from the gate, and dusted her hands off. If she hadn't gone after Marigold, Quintus wouldn't be lost now. But they could do no more for him. After reuniting with Rose and her mother, Lily had joined them in tracking the Greek man. They had spent nearly two hours calling his name, with no response. They even tried to use animal scouts to report his location, but he'd vanished without a trace during the time Lily had been chasing Marigold's specter.

Lily shook her head as she gestured to the world beyond the closed gate. The lamb bleated.

Rose sighed. "I know. But we can't leave the *ráth* open either." She looked toward the celebrations. "Come on. We should have some fun before tomorrow."

Tomorrow, they'd search for the missing Greek again.

They'd only taken a few steps, with the lamb following close behind, when something banged on the gate with such a thunderous sound, Lily didn't think it human.

A small moment of uneasy silence almost made her wonder if they'd imagined the banging, like how she imagined Marigold earlier.

Then the pounding came again.

The lamb bleated and scampered away into the darkness beyond the fires. Probably heading for the safety of their roundhouse.

The quiet that followed answered no questions, so Lily moved to the gate's wooden bar.

Rose reached out a hand but missed grabbing the edge of her cloak. So, she grabbed a nearby torch from its bracket on the palisade. "It couldn't be Quintus."

Reaching the gate, a wash of images swirled in Lily's mind. She saw herself, Rose, and Ciara. Other people came to her thoughts, but she didn't know them. Either way, it confused her.

Whatever was on the other side was definitely a land animal, and he seemed to know them. Something about him was familiar.

While she worked quickly to raise the wooden bar from its cradle, she sent images back to the creature on the other side, common pictures of warmth, like the sun and a warm spring. These images tended to calm nervous animals, which created a better interaction between her and the beasts.

Rose grabbed her arm. "What are you doing, Lil?"

Lily shook her off, sliding the heavy wooden bar to the side and then grabbing the gate handle.

Rose backed up but held the torch higher to illuminate the entrance.

As the doorway widened, a broad, shaggy head with fur as black as pitch poked through, towering over them.

Rose screamed and fell to the ground. The torch sputtered as it thudded against the damp earth, its fire diminishing, then winking out.

"Run, Lil!"

Even with Rose's reaction and the loss of immediate light, Lily remained calm. She knew the creature meant no harm, so she stood her ground until her vision adjusted to the light of a half moon, the glare of fires behind her casting wavering shadows.

The animal had moved through the gate, a giant at seven feet tall, standing on two legs as thick as small trees. He held his head up, nose smelling the air, which showed Lily a fairly straight profile from forehead to black nose tip. He almost looked like a dog.

A big dog.

On two legs.

Rose must have climbed to her feet because she grabbed Lily's arm again and leaned in close. "What is it?"

Lily tilted her head, trying to see the animal's features, but the light was not enough. She held up a hand toward him and clicked her fingers before turning her palm up. The great shaggy head swung her way. Slowly, the animal reached out a paw and laid it atop her outstretched hand. Nearly two-inch claws grazed the inside of her wrist.

The same flood of images filled her mind. They all contained people and very human objects. There was very little to suggest the forest or other animals. Lily sorted through the message and sent one of her own, letting him know he was welcomed, and then she gripped Rose's forearm to let her know he was safe.

No idea what he could be, but he was domesticated.

Who would tame such a large animal? None that she knew in the area.

Slowly, she withdrew her hand. New images hit her. A warm fire, a blanket, a bowl of food. *Venison?*

The message surprised her. The creature wanted shelter and sustenance like a human, but the image of meat made her uncomfortable. What if they were on the menu?

She must have conveyed her anxiety to the creature because he showed her an image of herself and Rose with what could only be an aura of companionship surrounding them. Lily gestured to their roundhouse deeper into the *ráth*, letting Rose see the signal as well.

"Don't be silly. He's not like your lamb."

With a quiet shrug, Lily closed the gate and set the wooden bar in place. Rose helped with a grunt of annoyance. Then, Lily clicked her fingers and took a few steps down a stone path raised above the muddy ground. She kept an eye on the dark shape of the animal. He huffed, lumbered a few steps forward, and then dropped down to all four paws, still nearly five feet high at his shoulders. It seemed two legs were not his normal stance as in only a couple of strides on his four legs, and he was by her side. Lily's eyes widened. He was fast for being so big.

"I don't understand you, Lil." Rose stretched her legs to catch up. "You scoff at the idea of a leprechaun, yet we talk with animals. You even let your *tíolacadh* guide you like now."

With a half smile, Lily shrugged, striding toward the wall's perimeter, away from the light of the fires. She took this circuitous route to avoid people as well.

However, someone spotted them, and a man's voice yelled out. "What manner of creature do you have there, Sneachta Bán and Rós Dearg?"

Lily peered inward to the central fire but couldn't see the speaker.

Then another voice rose to answer the first. "That's the biggest dog I ever did see."

A little fearful, Lily hastened past them. She didn't want anyone taking too close a look and finding the strange creature. No telling what would happen, but some would surely make sport, perhaps even antagonize the beast just to see his response.

But then two figures detached from the celebrations and intercepted them. Within moments, Lily distinguished the smaller stature of her mother and the self-assured one of Ana.

Both women gaped, but Ana spoke first. "That is not a dog."

The creature huffed, so Lily tentatively touched one of his round, fuzzy ears. He closed his eyes and tilted his head into her hand, a smoky floral scent wafted over her. Her heart filled with affection for the animal. She didn't know how or why but felt he would be good for her.

Although, she was inclined to agree with the *bandraoi*. He was not a dog, and Ana should know, because she had traveled extensively throughout Éire's lands.

Ciara clicked her tongue, pulling her cloak over her brown dress. "I know you think you have control of that creature, Lily, but he's a wild animal. We need to be careful."

Control? Lily raised an eyebrow, but Rose interjected.

"Mamaí, Lily has made a connection with him, so let her be."

Lily grinned at her sister. A moment ago, Rose didn't trust the creature either, but she would always defend Lily's choices. Her sister bounced on her feet again, peering past them to the singing and dancing.

Ana linked her hand with Ciara's, glancing down at the shorter woman. "I think we should hide the beast in the roundhouse."

Ciara nodded. "That's a good idea."

Exasperated, Lily blew her fine hair out of her eyes. That had been her intention before being stopped.

Swaying in place, Rose said, "While you do that, I'm going to celebrate Samhain." She twirled toward the central fire, then threw a serious look at Lily. "Tomorrow we find our missing Greek man."

CHAPTER 7

THE NEXT MORNING, LILY awoke when the beast moved away from where he had curled next to her all night, the scent of berries leaving with him out of the roundhouse. She gave him a few moments to take care of business while she brushed her hair with a bone comb, noticing Rose's pallet was already empty. Probably out for her morning run. Rose could outrun almost anyone, and she prided herself on the fact, constantly jogging her morning rounds.

Lily had just poured water into a wooden cup when the animal poked its head back into the roundhouse. His eyes widened at the sight of the cup, and he bounded to her side, the ground shaking with his heavy footfalls. Her mother groaned awake, and she untangled herself from Ana's longer limbs to watch the beast.

He sat on his hind legs and held up his two front paws. A long, pink tongue flicked out to lick his mouth, his request evident beyond the mental images.

Lily smirked as she handed him the cup.

It looked so small in his paws as he tried to balance it enough to bring it to his mouth, but the movement was awkward. She giggled as he tried to tip it up, the water barely making it into his mouth. Even Ciara chuckled at the sight as he rotated his head under the cup and stuck out his tongue, lapping more at air than water.

Lily put a hand on his front leg to communicate her message more effectively. *An Abhainn Bradán* coursed by *Ráth Bláthanna* just five minutes from the wooden palisade. Although cold, the water would be easier to drink.

The creature understood her well enough to follow her out of the

35

roundhouse. Pale fingers of a morning sun barely broke the horizon, the sky still dark. Mist lingered in the air, along with the smell of low-burning fires. A log crackled.

After gingerly scooting through the grounds of the *ráth*, avoiding numerous snoring lumps wrapped tight in fur blankets, Lily passed through the wooden gate, waving to Odhran's younger brother, Coilean, who stood watch at the top of the palisade. He gawked at seeing the beast.

When they reached the river, the beast took his fill. Meanwhile, she splashed water on her face. When he finished, he ambled toward her, then loomed up on two legs, placing huge paws on her shoulders. He grumbled low in his throat, as if trying to speak.

A stream of images rolled through her mind, coming so fast and strong that the world spun. She could barely make sense of what she saw, but they included men she didn't recognize and a stone house nearly as big as her *ráth*. By the time her vision cleared, the beast had lumbered away into the forest.

She sent a message, pleading for the creature to stop, but he moved farther into the dense woods. She chewed her lip, wanting to follow, but his missive had been clear. He meant for her to leave him be. She sighed. She had another mission, anyway—finding the Greek soldier.

Her day would be full.

With that decision, she met her family back inside the roundhouse and helped Rose gather supplies to last for at least two days, packing them into leather satchels to strap across their backs. No telling whether she or Rose would come across his tracks. Either way, they needed to avoid the *ráth* until their visitors left, unless they wanted to make a commitment for marriage.

Lily grimaced at the thought of marrying Dermot as she secured an extra spear in the harness on her back, carrying one in her hand. Rose strapped on her favored dagger and tied a sling with a bag of round stones to her belt. Both wore a man's long tunic, belted short at the waist, and a pair of trousers. While Rose was fond of her green dress, even she agreed with the need to attire more appropriately for their travels when Lily pushed a pair of trousers into her arms.

Ciara checked a fire-starter pouch, probably making sure it had enough flint and some hay or heather, then tied this to Rose's leather belt. "Be careful, girls."

Rose swung her thick woolen cloak around her shoulders and closed the clasp at her breast. "We only have to worry about the cold."

Lily grimaced, looking at the central hearth. She already missed the warm roundhouse.

With two hands, Ciara reached up to grip the edges of Rose's hood and pull it forward. "You need to worry about reavers and wolves, too." She cupped her cheek for a moment before turning to Lily.

Her mother eyed her, then pulled the frayed cloak ends closer together and adjusted the straps for her leather satchel. "Use your gifts to communicate with the animals to stay alert. Be aware of your surroundings at all times, and..." She wagged a finger at Lily. "No chasing ghosts."

Lily nodded, chastened, but Rose blew out her cheeks. "Of course, Mamaí. We should be back by the end of the second day at the latest. Hopefully most of our guests will be gone by then. And if we don't find the Greek soldier, he may not be alive."

The room seemed to spin for a moment, and Lily's chest ached. Looking for Quintus might be as useless as it had been to look for Marigold among the waves, but she would try. She was responsible for the Greek man being lost.

She glanced around the small roundhouse, her eyes lingering on the stall where Marigold's sleeping pallet still lay. She drew a deep breath. Part of her longed to curl up in a ball in her sister's blankets and forget the world.

She shook her head. Lingering on the past clouded the future.

And Quintus needed her. As Rose liked to say: *"Cha d'dhùin doras nach d'fhosgail doras."*

No door closed without another opening.

Rose grabbed her mother's hand. "May the good folk watch over us."

Lily released the breath she'd been holding, brushed past Rose, and walked out of the roundhouse.

They'd decided to trace their path back at the river, covering the distance in less than an hour. The sun now stood above the horizon. The day warmed faster than yesterday, the ground firmer. Wildlife's low hum trickled in the song of rushing water. Clear footprints from the day before overlapped in several directions.

Lily pointed to one section.

Rose nodded. "Longer and deeper boot prints. Quintus."

He'd followed her off the main path, heading westward where she'd followed Marigold's ghost. With a quick look at Rose, Lily tracked him as he veered off the path. They did this yesterday too, but they had lost all sign of him. Perhaps today they'd see something they had missed during the late afternoon light of the previous day.

A quarter of an hour later, they entered the clearing where Marigold's apparition had stopped and tried to talk to Lily. To the right was where Lily had fled when the eagle swooped at her. She ducked, thinking of the eagle, looking up into the tree boughs. No sign of the bird today. Tension left her shoulders.

"It doesn't seem the Greek followed you past the clearing."

Lily agreed. If he had, surely, he and Rose would have met up in trying to find her. Chewing her bottom lip, she followed the perimeter of the clearing, searching for something to give her a clue. Then she saw a small, crushed log. She crouched close to the ground, examining the wood. The log itself wasn't very big, maybe a half pace in diameter, but something heavy had stepped right on top of it, and the wood broke under the pressure, already decayed through the middle.

She'd bet it was Quintus.

Motioning for Rose to follow her, she took cautious steps forward, trying to locate any other traces. Then she spied his boot impression in a patch of soft, shadowed earth. After that, she knew she was on the right path. *But where was he going?*

After nearly another hour, the trail vanished. She huffed where she stopped, eyeing the brown grass.

Rose brushed past her to examine what appeared to be a scuffle among the scattered leaves and crushed twigs. The soldier's footsteps led right into it. "Where did the foolish man go?"

Lily bent to touch the ground. *Maybe an animal got him?* But there was no blood or any piece of him to indicate an attack.

Leaning forward to lay out on the earth, she scanned the top of the ground, following all the lines that disturbed the tiniest blade of grass, trying to imagine what had happened. She had seen a tracker do this once.

She clicked her tongue. Maybe if she were a better tracker, she'd be able to figure out something, but as it was, lying on the ground only made her cold.

She stood, brushing her hands off on her legs, then pumped her fingers into fists to loosen them, strengthening her grip on the spear again.

Now what?

She cocked her head, listening. Trickling water. Brush and leaves moving with animals of various sizes. A few birds braving the coming winter to sing a last song. A grunt echoed between the trees, followed by a heartrending cry. It came from the same direction as the water.

She shared a glance with Rose before dashing forward. Rose pulled ahead of her with her usual speed.

Her breath whooshed in her ears as she burst through the bush, using her spear to slash at thin spots in the foliage. She bounded through the forest's dense underbelly, trying to keep Rose in sight. A wane sun peeked through in spare moments, highlighting open paths for her. Her nostrils flared.

Following Rose, she tumbled into a grove of rowanberry trees. They rustled their orange and yellow leaves, cupping bright-red clusters of berries. The ground inclined slightly. At the summit, a well bubbled up to feed a small downward stream. Long grasses and moss clung to the submerged stones that circled the well's center. And next to the well, the little man, the ridiculously named leprechaun, struggled against an eagle.

The same eagle with a golden nape!

The large bird gripped the little man's coat in his talons, trying to carry him away by yanking him off the ground every few paces, but the man held fast to whatever his hands could reach. He screamed at the eagle.

Then Lily spied the great beast who'd slept next to her last night. He lumbered through the rowanberry trees and surged toward the small man on all four legs, looking so much like an oversized, rabid dog.

Rose sprinted to the man's aid. With no time for wonder, Lily caught up to her. Together, they grabbed the little man and yanked him from the eagle's grasp. The dog-like beast swiped a great clawed arm at the man. Lily ducked below the paw, gasping, dropping the little man.

Her sister spun away to avoid the beast as well, her satchel flinging to the ground. Then she turned a red face to him, her voice raised. "What is wrong with you?"

No one moved for a moment, with only the eagle's beating wings breaking the silence. Then the bird screeched and plunged at the little man again. The beast roared.

Lily threw herself between man and beast. She held her arms up, spear slanted to block his way while shooting warning messages to him. The black beast gave up and sat back on his haunches with a loud roar of frustration.

But the eagle ignored Rose's intervention and grasped the man once more. Rose caught the man and ripped him from the eagle's talons, his coat shredding. She shrieked at the eagle. "Leave him be."

The bird hovered in the air, his wings stirring the wind. He chirped rapidly, his eyes flickering from Rose to Lily. With a last whistle, he whirled to a low-hanging branch, settling down to watch them.

Lily sighed and gave her beast a stern look.

He swiped a paw at his nose, but didn't move otherwise, so she turned to the little man. He ran pudgy hands over his coat. Red splotches crossed his face, his bulbous nose the brightest. Large tears ripped clean through on both shoulders and one over his left breast, but no blood was visible.

He recovered by straightening his shoulders and yanking the bottom of his coat down. He glared at them. "Couldn't you have helped me more carefully? See my fine coat? You have damaged it so that it is all torn and full of holes, you clumsy creatures!" His voice cracked as it raised higher while yelling at them.

Lily crossed her arms, mouth set in a tight line, but Rose didn't hold her tongue this time. "You are an ungrateful thing, aren't you?"

He ignored her as he looked around him, searching in the tall grasses for something. His little body weaved through the brush.

"Your coat can be mended, unlike your life."

"Aha!" He seemed to find what he was looking for, and Lily peered at what he gathered into a small leather bag. Precious stones of nearly every rainbow color littered the ground. When he collected them all, he looked at Rose. "Mend my coat?"

Rose nodded. He waded back toward her.

Something prickled Lily's hair. The feeling snaked up her arms and along the back of her neck. The beast next to her leaned forward, a growl rumbling in his chest.

She raised an eyebrow at him. *Maybe he was a dog.*

Then, in a movement too quick for Lily to completely follow, the strange little man withdrew something from his coat and touched it to Rose. Light blinded the entire area, and she threw her hand over her eyes. When the spots cleared, Rose was gone. The little man clutched a small, reddish-brown mouse in his hand, which he quickly stowed away in a front coat pocket.

Then he leapt into the well.

Lily lunged after him, too late. He sunk below the waters and out of sight.

CHAPTER 8

FEAR SLAMMED HER to a standstill.

Marigold had disappeared in water.

Then a whooshing wind of wings brushed her cheek as the eagle dove into the well, gone within seconds.

Great Mother Goddess!

Uneasiness squirmed in her stomach as she peered into the well, thinking to see the bird drowned. But he was gone. She swallowed against the bile rising in her throat. She couldn't tear her eyes from the water as it cascaded out from deep within, rolling forward into the gurgling stream.

What just happened?

Did the small man turn Rose into a mouse? There didn't seem to be another explanation. Rose was there one minute, gone the next, and a mouse had appeared.

Magic.

She bit her tongue hard, tasting metallic blood.

And the eagle? Surely it drowned.

Along with Rose, if Rose had been the mouse. Swallowed by the water, just like Marigold.

Lily dropped to her knees, ignoring the rocky bank digging into her legs through her trousers. The beast sidled next to her and laid a paw on her back. The very human pat surprised her, but her thoughts soon turned back to her sister.

Was Rose still alive? Under the water...

She had to be.

Lily replayed every moment since entering the grove.

Then shook her head.

She didn't even know where Rose had gone except into the well. But surely they weren't still in the water. Even the leprechaun needed air to breathe. So that meant the well led somewhere.

When had she started to think of the small man as a leprechaun?

She rubbed her arms. Perhaps since he had transformed her sister into a mouse, then vanished into a well along with the eagle. Even the beast sniffed at the well, extending a paw to pull himself up to look inside, as if wondering her same thoughts.

None of it made sense.

She shivered, blinking rapidly at the gurgling water. An outlandish idea came to her.

A portal to somewhere else. The Otherworld.

What did the stories say?

She rubbed fingers across her tight forehead.

Samhain allowed portals to open, making it easier to access the Otherworld. But when the day ended at sunset, what happened then?

She rubbed her eyes. *Have I gone mad?*

With a sigh, she stood, gathering her courage to descend the waters of the well, feeling dizzy the moment she stepped forward. The world tilted up. She held out her arms to steady herself, but when she took a step into the water, she froze.

She hadn't consciously entered any body of water since Marigold. Knowing her only remaining sister was in trouble should have been enough to push her forward, but her body refused to cooperate.

She whimpered. Then stepped back.

Where was her courage? Would she really lose another sister because she couldn't face her fear?

She dug her fingernails into her palms.

Move!

But she didn't.

A flash of light appeared from the corner of her eye. She spun toward it, relieved to turn away from the water, then jerked. The black beast jolted as well.

Marigold, wearing all white and encircled in a warm glow, stood before her. She appeared more beautiful than ever. A golden band on her forehead weighed down her yellow curls. A wide belt of the same metal lay along her hips and a golden chain hung on her neck. They had never owned such wealth before.

Lily reached a hand to her sister. But Marigold swept out of reach, her light-colored eyes pleading with her as she floated out of the grove, motioning her to follow, so Lily numbly complied.

A part of her yelled to go back. Back to the well where Rose disappeared, but she couldn't ignore Marigold.

No, that was only partly true. Relief loosened a tight ball in her chest the further away she moved from the water.

Coward!

So, she scrambled after her dead sister, breaking thin branches and slashing at bushes every few paces, yet nothing disrupted Marigold's shimmering image as it glided ahead.

The beast also left a wide path as he lumbered behind Lily. She'd find her way back to the well easily enough. For now, she kept her sights on Marigold and wondered whatever happened to her simple life, one without so much magic.

CHAPTER 9

MARIGOLD OUTPACED HER, not bothered by the denser parts of the forest and rising landscape. Nothing disturbed in her wake.

Lily's breath came loud in her ears, but she pushed on through the stitch forming in her left side, sweat pooling between her breasts. She attempted to swallow past the lump in her throat. She couldn't let fear overcome her, but losing Rose crept back into her mind no matter how many times she tamped it down.

Fear wormed toward despair. Tears blurred her vision.

She would not lose Rose.

That's why she followed her dead sister through the woods now. Somehow, she knew Marigold meant to help, and maybe that didn't involve water.

She plugged fingers into her eyes to push the tears away, then swiped at the sweat on her forehead. An early winter wind reached through some parts of the forest, and she thanked the cool air. In these same parts, the sun showed her that almost half the morning had passed. She worried about the timing. If the well was a portal, it would only stay open until sunset.

Could she force herself into the waters by then?

She gulped against the burning in her throat.

Steeper slopes soon replaced the gradual incline as she neared the beginnings of a rocky mountain. A quick breeze swept through as trees thinned their ranks. The black beast trudged on all fours, next to her now. Every so often, she marked a tree with her spear and noted the position of the sun.

She would not lose Rose.

An outcrop of rock and large boulders appeared ahead. For a moment, Marigold stood below the rocky barrier, and then suddenly stood atop the outcrop before climbing higher. Her light continually shone between the trees as she meandered through them.

Then, for the first time since reappearing, she was gone. With a maddening cry, Lily hurried. Climbing the rocky path would take far more time than it had for her ghostly sister.

She rubbed away sweat dripping into her eyes and plodded on. Once, she slid back on loose rocks, and the beast caught her with a paw on her backside and pushed her forward. With a blush, she sent him a message of thanks. He seemed steadier on his four legs. Long claws dug into the ground with each step, although the images he sent her showed strong legs ending in sturdy boots.

A small smile turned up her lips. Boots would have been better than the simple leather shoes she wore, but she'd climbed many of the hills and mountains in the area with the same shoes. Although she'd never been chasing someone.

Stalking dinner, but never chasing.

Finally, she reached the top of the rocky outcrop. She stopped to catch her breath and gazed out at the view down the slopes and across the top of the forest. Brilliant autumn colors shone beneath an afternoon sun. A gorgeous sight meant to bring peace.

No peace today. Fear tugged at her heart.

Why had Marigold brought me here?

Taking one last deep breath, she jogged into the forest behind her, the beast lumbering along. She hadn't advanced too far before hearing a hacking sound, a long cough filled with fluid. She diverted toward the noise but slowed as she neared the source. The beast crashed next to her, and she held up a hand to steady him, sending him a message to stay and watch her back.

She crept forward in a crouch, reaching for one of her spears, until the trees thinned near a cave. Sidling closer, she dropped to the ground and crawled until she could peek through a small opening in a thick bush.

Before her lay a small campsite, a fire started at the opening of the cave. Something roasted over the fire. She sniffed the air. Rabbit.

But where were the people?

Then a man emerged from the cave, a walking stick in one hand. Lily recognized him from the *ráth* yesterday. He had been the old man who had dozed next to a fire while crouching over a wooden staff. Now, he sat at his own fire.

What was he doing out here alone? She hadn't noticed him leaving the *ráth*, but then she had been preoccupied with finding the missing Greek and hiding the creature now at her side.

A tingling sensation crawled up her arms. She steadied herself before standing up and walking into the campsite. Marigold had brought her here for a reason. The old man was important.

He looked up at her approach with one gray eye, the other covered by a patch. His bald head sported a few stray silver strands flopping about in the wind. He smiled, showing gums mostly devoid of teeth. "Did the leprechaun visit you again, girl?"

She jerked at the unexpected question.

The old man laid a finger along his nose. "I heard the stories yesterday. But why are you here visiting me?"

Clearing her throat from persistent disuse, she crouched down across from him, the fire between them. Her voice cracked. "Help me find my sister."

With the smell of berries, her black beast hunkered down next to her, and the man eyed him with curiosity before responding. "Why would I do that?"

And why would he? Lily used her spear tip to trace circles in the dirt around the fire. Marigold knew the answer.

Then it came to her, and she regarded him with a steely calm. He'd clearly heard the story of their encounter and then left the safety of their settlement, which could be dangerous for such an old man alone in the wilderness. She pointed the spear tip toward him. "You're looking for the leprechaun."

He chewed the corner of his lip before bursting out with a loud laugh. He slapped his thigh with a hand. "You're a clever girl, aren't you?"

Tight-lipped, she gave a quick nod. "He took my sister."

"Well, if I'm to help you, at least you should know my name. I know yours, Líle níc Muaich." He tapped his eye patch with her quick surprise. "And me, I'm Fintan mac Bóchra." He hesitated a moment before continuing, as if waiting for her reaction.

Lily thought the name sounded familiar.

Shrugging, Fintan picked up a stick. The fire dimmed as he shifted burning twigs beneath the roasting rabbit. He dropped the stick and rubbed his hands together. "Let's eat first, then you and your bear can show me where the leprechaun disappeared."

Lily rocked back on her feet, a hand on her belly as she glanced at her furry companion. The beast held a small branch of overripe rowanberries, his teeth pulling off clusters to munch on.

A bear?

Dogs certainly didn't eat berries, but how did a bear come to be here? There hadn't been one seen in these lands for thousands of years. Surely the old man must know a lot about the world to have recognized the animal.

He handed her a piece of torn rabbit, and she nibbled on it. Then tilted her head while sucking the juices on her fingers, eyeing the stranger. Who was this man with such knowledge, and why would he agree to help her? "Why are you looking for the leprechaun?"

Fintan angled his head, studying her with his one eye. "He took something from me."

She wanted to ask what the leprechaun had taken, but her throat felt raw with her recent talking. Plus, the old man savored his meat, closing his one eye.

Would he tell her the truth anyway? He was a stranger, after all, even if she had to trust him now.

These thoughts tumbled through her mind as they made quick work of the rabbit meal. Then together they cleared the campsite before starting their trek toward the well. Lily tried to fill her mind with any other reflections to distract herself from the idea of the well, a way to avoid thinking about descending into the water, which flipped her insides all around.

For one of his age with a walking stick, the old man matched her steady pace easily enough. The bear brought up the rear, a great rumbling sound from deep in his chest increasing as they neared the well.

Behind her, Fintan tapped his walking staff on the ground a bit harder, grabbing her attention. "Curious," he said. "How did you find me?"

She spoke, breathless, over her shoulder. "My sister."

"You have another sister?" He paused, as if looking around, which caused her to halt. "Where is she?"

Lily resumed walking, gripping her spear shaft tighter. "Dead."

She wasn't much used to talking anymore and particularly didn't like speaking to strangers. It was made worse to have to speak of Marigold. She wanted to spit out the disgust in her mouth but stopped short of it when she broke into the clearing with the well.

Her breath stilled in her chest.

Fintan halted next to her, almost as tall as her even hunched over his staff. He scratched a finger over his lined cheek. "You talk to dead sisters and see leprechauns. Anything else you can do?"

She expelled her breath while her cheeks heated, and she shrugged a hand at the bear lumbering toward the well. "Talk to him."

He peered at her with his one gray eye. "Curious. The gods are merciful with those who are special."

She didn't know what that meant and thought him a strange man. However, she had to trust that Marigold knew what she was doing to have brought her to him.

Fintan wrapped his worn, wool cloak close to his body and moved to the well, peering down into the gurgling waters. "Nice. A ladder will make this easy."

Lily hadn't moved any closer. Fear froze her in place.

"What's the matter with you, girl?"

She squeezed her eyes shut and shook her head. The silence that followed was only broken by the bear's moan. Time was slipping away as the old man awaited her response, so she took a deep breath. "My sister drowned."

When she looked up at Fintan, empathy clearly reflected in his one eye. He toddled back to her with his walking staff and laid a hand on her shoulder. "I know the loss you feeling and sure that I lost sixteen wives and all my children in a flood."

Furrowing her brow, she responded in a near whisper. "What did you do?"

He smiled his gummy grin. "Nothing else I could do about it. I turned into a fish."

A sudden laugh pulled from the depth of her soul, and she placed a hand over her nervous belly. She glanced at the well. "I can't do this."

His fingers tightened over her shoulders. "You can let your loss define you by dictating your cowardice, or you can let it make you stronger."

She rubbed the back of her neck. *Could I be stronger?*

Bile climbed her throat, and she swallowed. She dropped her satchel to the ground alongside the one Rose had lost. She withdrew a wrapped oatcake, taking a bite, hoping to settle her stomach, her throat aching and raw.

Life would be unbearable if she lost Rose, too.

With all her thoughts and feelings flipping somersaults in her belly, she found herself walking to the well, nibbling the oatcake. The ladder stood steady on the inside of the stone ring where water burst forth.

If she died, would it matter?

Without Rose and Marigold, she didn't want to live in the world anyway. Her sisters had been her best friends, the ones who knew her so well and loved her unconditionally. Her sisters were only different sides of her own being. Nothing could ever replace the bond they shared.

Bolstered, she licked her fingers clean and harnessed her spear. She eyed her satchel but didn't think the contents would survive a complete submerging. She was also afraid it would weigh her down in the water.

With a final deep breath, she waded in, sloshing over stones. Cold water seeped through her clothes, and she shivered.

A thought surfaced.

What about Mamaí, Ana, and Nana? She shook her head. If she lost Rose, her grief would be too great. She'd go crazy.

She looked at Fintan as she lowered herself to the first rung of the ladder. He smiled with encouragement, and she marveled at him. He'd lived his whole life with his grief. Sixteen wives? *And children?*

The bear peered over the old man's shoulder, his muzzle sniffing the air. Lily finally recognized an emotion that often came through the bear's messages. He had lost someone, too.

She sunk lower into the freezing water, her feet feeling for the next step.

Then another thought struck her.

She met Fintan's eye. "I remember your story." Her mother's words floated in her memories. The countless tales of Éire and the Otherworld. "You were one of the first to settle here. You married Noah's granddaughter. That's who you lost. But that was nearly five thousand years ago..."

She didn't have time to finish her thought as Fintan pushed her down. Her feet slipped on the next rung, and she submerged the rest of the way into the water, gulping just a last bit of air before. Then she fought. She fought not to choke in water. She fought to keep moving, to push her body down the next rung of the ladder. The world darkened around her within a few feet, and she fought against the panic of a senseless world. Only the cold and darkness surrounded her. Pressure built in her chest as the need for air grew stronger.

Just when she thought she'd have to breathe, her head broke up through the water's surface.

Up?

It made no sense. If she had been going down, how was she now coming up through the water?

Even with the thought, she quickly pulled herself out of the well, tumbling to the warm ground on the other side of the circular stone wall. She coughed against the bright blades of grass, gasping for breath. Her fingers dug into the earth.

Was this the Otherworld? Water dripped into her eyes, so she squeezed them shut. She wasn't sure what was real or not anymore.

Within moments, Fintan stood next to her. He seemed unbothered by his trip through the well. His long tunic was soggy. Water dripped from his bushy eyebrows. She sat up, sucking in a deep breath as she eyed him. He reminded her of a wet cat, all bones sticking out and much smaller wet than with dry fur.

Then the bear emerged. He huffed and sneezed several times. He shook all over, sending a spray of water over them. Lily shrieked from the surprise shower, and Fintan glowered at the animal.

A warm breeze kissed her cheeks. She turned her head to the sun. It was a midday summer sun, not fall. Pillar stones slanted shadows over her.

As she craned her neck higher, she saw the sky end above the sun in a line of water. It was as if she had stood on the beach and gazed across the ocean and the sun above it, except it was upside-down.

Where had they gone?

As if sensing her question, Fintan spread his arms wide, staff in one hand, and lifted his chin to the sky. "Welcome to *Tir fo Thuinn*, the Land under the Wave."

CHAPTER 10

GLASS WINDOWS AND WALLS shimmered when the morning sun peered through the treetops. Lugh particularly loved how the glass melded seamlessly with the rock face of the mountain where his cave opened. Once upon a time, his home had just been the small cave. Eventually, he had built something grand out of it.

Shifting his bag of gems on his shoulder, he entered through the glass door, an opening nearly four times as tall as his small body. There was no one to welcome him or announce his return home. But he preferred that.

Or did he?

He frowned. *Wasn't there someone to meet him once?*

He breezed through the rooms. One had a loom that spun gold. Large bales of the precious metal stacked to the ceiling. Another room held boiling cauldrons of wax and candles drying above them. The next also held huge vats of boiling liquid, and Lugh licked his lips at the smell of the ales brewing.

The next room held well over a hundred shoes in various states of disrepair. Tools littered the floor and workbenches. Another hosted musical instruments such as various small harps and a larger harp with thirty strings, a timpan, a dord or bronze horn, a fife, several flutes, a guthbuinne or a bassoon-type horn, hornpipes, and a sturgan or trumpet.

Still another stored a vast array of weapons. Spears of varying lengths and colors and one with five points, some with decorated spearheads. Skeans or double-edged daggers, a forked javelin, flint knives, and axes. Against one wall was a black shield with a hard boss of white bronze.

Then, in the very center on its own pedestal stood a harp with three strings of different metals—iron, bronze, and silver. The harp itself was made from oak and richly decorated with a double headed fish design, studded with jeweled eyes.

But he passed these rooms. He only stopped when he came to the most cavernous room in his home. Part of its ceiling was glass, the other half the beginning of what used to be the small cave. He'd carved the cave out so that it could swallow the glass part of his house now.

He drew in a deep breath with a smile. Nice to be home.

Next, he moved further into the cave, plunging into darker depths which housed the treasures and baubles found in his travels, along with a housemate that sometimes helped him. Here he dumped his bag of precious jewels atop a mound of other gems and gold and silver coins.

Paiste, the black-scaled dragon raised his head. Twin smoky fumes leaked from his wide nostrils. "New fortunes!"

Lugh hopped from one foot to the other. "More to come, but you have to be on the lookout for strangers coming from the well."

The dragon puffed a ring of smoke up to the ceiling where it encircled a stalactite. "I'll hunt."

Lugh returned his curling smile. One of the tunnels somewhere in here led up out of the mountain. Lugh had never found it, but Paiste knew it.

After tossing the bag aside, Lugh ventured back to the cave opening where melded glass welcomed natural sunlight into the sparse room. A thud drew his eye skyward, and he jumped nearly out of his skin.

Bloody eagle!

It had followed him, and now the revolting creature had landed on the glass roof, his head moving side to side to peer down at him with beady eyes. The bird pecked at the glass.

Bang, bang.

"Scram! Go mind your own business."

Lugh raised his hands, but remembering his shorn beard, lowered them. "Not worth the effort," he said.

Instead, he went to the central hearth where a kettle hung over several large sticks and started to lay out what he needed to stoke the dying fire.

Bang, bang.

Lugh hunched his shoulders and grit his teeth, ignoring the pesky bird. He stirred the big cauldron. Leftover stew.

Bang, bang.

He dropped the spoon, ready to yell, but then quickly gained his composer again. With the spoon, he lifted some of the stew out, regarding the contents. Carrots, onion, cabbage, and other vegetables. What he wouldn't give for some meat.

Bang, bang.

This time he threw the spoon aside and shook a fist at the eagle.

"Alright! May Dagda break your bones, you feathered nuisance."

He reached into his coat pocket and withdrew the mouse.

She curled asleep in his palm, so small. Her lovely reddish-brown fur shimmered. Gently, he laid her upon the rock floor. Then using the Druid rod, he touched her so that she transformed back into the girl she had been.

Lugh bent close to her head, red curls covering face. He hooked a curl and pulled it away, but before he let it go, he marveled at the silkiness of it.

His heart pulsed faster, sweat gathering along his mouth as he grit his teeth.

With carelessness, he yanked the hair from her face, a few strands breaking free. She groaned, but her eyes remained closed.

He frowned.

With an open palm, he smacked her cheek.

That woke her.

Bright blue eyes stared at him, bewildered, and then she scooted away from him. He stood up to his full height of nearly three paces. "Finally, sleeping harpy."

Those eyes look hurt as she rubbed the bright handprint on her face. "Do you have no manners?"

He puffed out his cheeks and pulled his beard forward. "You're no innocent mouse."

Then he dropped his beard and waved his hands toward her, his fingers wiggling. A golden glow emanated from his beard. The girl slid back to the rock wall to his right and chains appeared around her left foot, anchoring her to the wall with only a few feet slack. Her eyes widened.

He shrugged out of his torn jacket and threw it at her. She cried out as it hit her in the face. She hurriedly drew it down. Fire seemed to leap from her eyes now.

He grinned. "You owe me."

She sighed, giving up her anger, then bent her head to examine the jacket. He went back to the stew. Hopefully it'd be warm soon. He imagined a tasty hunk of deer added to the liquid and licked his lips.

"How am I to fix this?"

Popped out his reverie, he glared at her.

She poked one finger through the tear in the fabric. "I don't have magic like yours. I need needle and thread that matches the color."

With a noisy exhale, he waved a hand so that the supplies she asked for appeared next to her amid a golden glow. He continued to stir the stew but watched her out of the corner of his eye. Her nimble fingers measured out thread, cutting with her teeth, before slipping a length through the needle's eye. She seemed competent enough. Maybe he'd share a bowl of stew.

Of course, you will, Lugh.

He'd be an idiot not to. After all, she'd die without food, so he had to feed her. He stomped his foot. He didn't have to like it, though.

Bang, bang.

Rage boiled inside his chest, bursting forth. He shook his fist at the eagle above. "Dilberry maker!" Then he turned and kicked the wall. Anger dulled the pain lancing up his leg.

"He only wants to help."

Yanking on his beard, he turned to the girl, heat crawling up his neck. Her face tilted up to the glass ceiling, a smile curling her lips at the eagle. The sun lit fire in her curls. His anger lessened, but just a little. "What nonsense you speak." He set about drawing his wooden rocking chair to the hearth's heat.

"You want to add meat to the soup?" The needle worked across one tear, closing the two sides together.

"Now you know my mind, silly mouse?" He touched a finger to his temple with a snarl on his lips.

"My name is Rose."

"Who cares?" He crossed his arms as he sat in the rocking chair.

"I do, or should I call you grumpy leprechaun?" She flashed a look at him before returning to the coat.

"Argh!"

She should fear him.

But when he looked at her, she gave him a level stare, her voice low when she spoke. "No need for a temper." When he smashed his lips together, she paused in her sewing. "Look, if I am to be… let's say a guest, while I'm here, we might as well see if we can get along."

A guest?

No, she was his prisoner. She was his. Somehow, that made him feel superior. "You will do as I say."

"Sure. That's what I'm here for." She bent over the thread to capture it in her mouth and bite through it.

He realized he hadn't provided scissors. He let that thought fade away, even if a part of him felt guilty.

She flashed those blue eyes at him. "But I will help you."

He snorted. "How's that?"

"Let the eagle be my companion."

So, the girl felt something for the bird. Lugh could almost understand that. Like his pup, Failinis. But why should she have a pet when his was missing.

That's right!

It was his dog who usually met him when he arrived home. How could he have forgotten?

He slammed a fist on his leg as he stood. "I gave you what you needed to fix my coat." He stomped toward her. "What more do you want of me, Mousie?"

With a calm he certainly didn't feel, she set the coat down in her lap and met his eyes. "The eagle will bring you a rabbit for your stew. Then you'll let him stay with me."

And bloody rabbits' feet, that's just what he did.

CHAPTER 11

IN A CIRCLE OF PILLAR STONES, one stone stood taller than the others near a great tree laden with fruit. Beside this taller pillar-stone was the spring well with a large, round pool as clear as crystal. Water bubbled from the center and flowed away toward the middle of a flowery plain in a slender stream. The flowery plain ended in a forest of red yew trees.

Lily shrugged off the wool cloak, folding it up to store in the harness on her back. Summery perfumes tickled her nose as she marveled at the vastly different world.

Was Rose somewhere nearby?

A glitter caught her attention. She held a hand over her eyes, blocking the sun's glare. In the distance, some type of structure sprawled right out of the pleasant hills and forest.

"The royal palace," Fintan said. Tall houses with glittering roofs surrounded the palace. "Belongs to the king of this land, the Warrior of the Well." He ran a hand over his mostly bald head, wiping away water droplets. "We had better move before he comes. He's not one for visitors without his say-so."

The old man hobbled in the opposite direction of the palace, toward three mountains sitting deep in the red yew tree forest.

Lily spied the faint footprints he followed.

She chewed the corner of her lip before grasping her spear and following him. She was used to being the lead, but Fintan wanted to track the leprechaun as much as she did.

The bear fell to all four paws and lumbered beside her. His wet muzzle nudged her hand while he sent her an image of two people holding hands. Their faces were fuzzy, but the emotion stirred a feeling of support, so she ran her fingers through the fur on his head and rubbed an ear. He grumbled in contentment, and she smiled. His company soothed her.

As they entered the forest of yew trees, she tentatively sent her thoughts forward, seeking the minds of the land animals. *Would her gift work the same here?*

Her caution meant slow progress, but what would this world offer? She tried to recall the myriad stories her mother told.

The Otherworld had similar animals like those from Éire, but she thought she remembered tales of more fantastical creatures. But, as the images of deer, rabbits, squirrels, and other small critters filled her mind, she quirked a shoulder.

This could be her own forest back home except for the upside-down ocean and opposite season.

As the hours slipped by, she kept track of the animals' images, looking for their reflections of the tiny man. Fintan followed his physical tracks. At some point, the old man halted them by a small stream so they could refill their waterskins. Silver-blue salmon swam just out of reach, but one with an orange spot on its side sidled closer, its eyes tilting in curiosity.

Marigold could have communicated with the fish, maybe enticing it to come within reach. Lily wished it would swim just a bit closer. Hunger gnawed at her stomach. The shared rabbit had not been enough. With a sigh, she backed away, only to get splashed as the bear pounced through the water, desperate arms flailing for the salmon.

He looked awkward and clumsy in his pursuit, until Lily sent him an image of her leaving. This caught his attention. He huffed and bounded out of the water, paws empty. He directed a few choice images her way that spoke of his frustrations and his own hunger.

She pointed to the small red berries in the yew trees, and he eagerly grasped a cluster of them.

After they had spent several hours traveling, she glanced up through the boughs of the trees. The sun had not moved in the sky, but the light was weaker. The ocean above them had darkened, lending a twilight quality to the atmosphere. Lily would have guessed that they had spent the whole day traveling, but it was hard to tell when the sun didn't trace a path through the sky—or ocean, as that was what was above them.

Fintan peered up with her. "Time moves differently here and between the realms."

A fin abruptly broke the water's surface directly above her. Water spouted from a blowhole, before the fin disappeared back beneath the waves. For a moment, she couldn't move. *How was this even possible?* An upside-down ocean. A whole world swimming, living, breathing, eating above her head.

She flexed her fingers. Her stomach quivered from more than hunger now. How would she ever find Rose in this strange world?

But surely her sister was still alive.

She couldn't believe in any other possibility.

Finally, she pulled herself away from the sight, and they began their trek once more. The next stream they came to, she considered the fish again. Perhaps she could spear one. It was a hard task, especially with low light. Just as she raised her arm, she spotted the silver salmon with the orange spot on his side.

How had the creature changed streams?

She backed away from the flowing river, scanning the bank, the litter of rocks, the one tree edged close enough to send a root into the water. It was all familiar. She bumped into Fintan, then pointed to the familiar territory.

He slapped a hand to his forehead. "We're walking in circles. Wily leprechaun." He leaned more on his staff, shoulders drooped forward. He muttered under his breath.

Suddenly, a roar vibrated the trees' leaves, and the ground shook as if a very large man pounded the earth. Lily caught her balance and tightened her fingers on the spear. Fintan stiffened his back, the bear growled low in his throat, and they all turned toward the awful sound. Branches crashed to the ground as a large serpentine animal burst upon them, halting a dozen paces away.

Thick, black scales covered the sinuous body that stretched at least twenty-five paces long. Several pairs of legs ended in glinting talons and ram horns curled on the hideous head.

Lily's mouth slackened, her body shaking and her hands clenching.

Was that a dragon?

In that moment of her confusion, the creature charged. Fintan and the bear split from her, and the dragon aimed for her, nearly bowling her over as she dove toward the ground. Above her, a thin, forked tongue tasted the air. Hot breath washed over her face. In the next second, she rolled a few paces away, missing the chomp of slimy teeth. Then she pushed up to one knee, brought her spear back, and sent it forward.

It clinked off the dragon's head.

The monster blinked. His lips curled back in a slow smile, showing large, curved teeth covered with mucous slime. A smoky fire rumbled in the back of its throat while its yellow eyes gleamed. Lily threw up an arm over her face, waiting for the last few moments of her life.

Then the dragon's head snapped up in a tortured yowl. Blood fell in a torrent from a large arrow embedded in the creature's nose.

A jingle threaded through the dragon's painful growls. Musical notes started high and gently moved to a lower register before tripping high again. It was almost haunting.

Lily dropped her arm, astounded.

The dragon closed his eyes. The large body weaved in time to the music, then it slithered back into the depths of the forest. Lily released a long-held breath, then fell forward on her hands, her chin dropping to her chest. Her arms quivered.

Never had she been so close to her own death.

Then music penetrated the haze of her mind. She climbed to her feet and snatched her fallen spear, spinning in the direction of the chords. A recessed darkness between a ring of trees showed the faint outline of a tall creature. It took a step forward, revealing the face of a young boy blowing a set of wooden pipes lashed together. Naked to the waist, his bottom half was covered in gleaming brown fur and ended in horse's hooves. A large bow slung across his shoulders, with a quiver of arrows.

He towered over Lily as he moved closer to her, smiling around the pipes as he fully revealed himself. Thick, black hair curled around his dark face and black-rimmed ears, while the rest of him was a bay horse's body, complete with a dark tail. He finished a final round of notes with a boyish grin, then lowered the pipes. "Hallo."

Lily raised her spear in front of her.

The boy held out an arm, alarm raising his eyebrows. "Wait! I won't hurt you."

Slowing her movements, she tilted her head at him, just as Fintan and the black bear came back into the clearing. Clearing her scratchy throat, she asked, "What are you?"

"I'm Daric the centaur."

She swallowed her disbelief and lowered her spear, nodding. "Lily."

The old man stopped close to her and leaned on his staff. "We're thankful for your help, Daric."

A bright smile spread over his chubby cheeks as they reddened. He was missing a front tooth.

How old was the boy? Lily glanced around for others. Surely the child's parents would be nearby.

Maybe things worked differently in the Otherworld.

Fintan rubbed the whiskers on his face. "It seems we've been caught in a circle set by the leprechaun."

Daric giggled. "Yes, he likes to play tricks." He stuck out his tongue. "He's not that nice."

"We are trying to find him."

The centaur boy hooted. "Not very likely!" He sobered at Lily's glower. "Maybe my folks can help you. Want to come over for dinner?"

CHAPTER 12

LUGH HELD OUT HIS COAT. Grudging admiration stuck in his chest. He'd never say, but the stitching was good, pulling the fabric a little. The girl had added an overlay with a gold-colored thread to insert a unique design.

Her laugh pulled his attention, and he scowled.

From where she sat, the girl bowed her head, a smile lighting her face while she whispered to that bloody eagle again. The bird shifted on his feet in front of her, and then mimicked her, bowing his head.

The insufferable mouse sure didn't act like she was still chained to the wall. "Quiet all that racket before I turn you back into a rodent and let the eagle play with you."

That shut the hole in her face. He sniggered. Then he went about his tidy glass house, gathering tools and candles and putting them into a sack. He tamped down the hearth's fire and pulled on his best shoes for working. The girl's huge blue eyes followed his movements. He ignored her until he was done. Then he stood in front of her, hand on his beard. "You be going with me."

Long, slender fingers pulled a thread free on her light-green tunic, her eyes downcast, and then she looked up through pale lashes at him. "Where are you taking me?"

He stamped his foot. "Don't be coy, silly nit."

She was far too pretty for his tastes. He withdrew his Druid rod and touched it to her nose before she got out half a squeak. This time she shrunk in size to match his height. He smiled. The perfect male-female leprechaun, resplendent in a red coat over a flat chest, black trousers over wide hips, and a bright-red beard to match her flowing curly locks. Her large man-hands cupped her whiskered face and she shrieked.

He laughed so hard his stomach hurt, and he fell over. He rolled on the ground, hugging his sides. "Now you not so much a silly-looking oaf."

"But I'm a man!"

He got back to his feet, wiping away a tear. "No, gobermouch, just a leprechaun." He stowed away the magical rod in his coat and yanked her beard, dragging her off the floor.

"Ow!" She stumbled to her feet.

The eagle hopped on his taloned feet and emitted a high-pitched whistle.

"Harrumph! Now you know how it feels to have your beard messed with." Then he muttered under his breath as he looked her up and down. "Better to look at, too." Next, he hauled out his broom and had them sit astride the handle with her behind him. "Hold tight, gooseberry grinder."

He shot a mean look at the eagle. He'd lose the noxious bird in a moment.

They soared right through the glass walls. The silly mouse shrieked again and buried her face against his back. They hurtled over the forest under a twilight sun and zoomed straight up to the upside-down ocean. He tilted his face to the rushing wind, closed his eyes, and smiled before merging with the water.

Only mere seconds passed before they emerged into a night-shadowed land. The broom continued to zip through the cloudless sky, its destination relayed by Lugh's slightest hand signals. Although he knew this land with its rolling green hills and jagged coastlines, he wondered how much the girl knew beyond the peninsula of her settlement. She'd likely see more in tonight's trip than ever before. Although she may not recognize much in the darkness.

Above one sprawling homestead, he leveled the broom, coming first to the largest of roundhouses. A dog barked, tweaking his heart. He missed his dog.

No matter.

He landed and twitched his beard, which created a magical barrier, concealing them from the dog or any other late-night wanderer. He grabbed the girl's hand, hefting his sack on the other shoulder. The broom he left, and it hovered in anticipation of being called.

He stepped through the leather door flap, yanking the girl forward. She gave a small cry, which he hushed with a finger to his lips. Tiptoeing around the inside perimeter, Lugh did his best to avoid the sleeping. This roundhouse was large enough to have several stalls filled with people, oblivious to him as he sifted through their shoes. He piled a few into the girl's arms. Then, with a faint golden glow from his beard, he shoved her to the side of the roundhouse, her terrified shriek dying as she passed right through the wooden wall without harm.

He snuck across the open plain, heading inside a lean-to supported by a large boulder. Salted meat hung on hooks from the wooden ceiling planks, a pile of deer skins rested on the floor, and in the middle, two wooden barrels stood side by side. He climbed a log next to one of the barrels, finding a ladle hooked on the side. He dipped it into the dark-colored liquid and drank deeply. The ale hit the back of his throat with a warm tingle, and he sighed.

"Drop those shoes, Mousie, and come get some of this."

She climbed the log and tentatively took a sip. After swirling the ale in her mouth and swallowing, she drank more, ladle after ladle. Dark liquid pearls rolled down the wiry red hairs of her beard.

Lugh chuckled before leaving her to it. He dug through his sack for the right tools and then went to work on the shoes.

These were once refined shoes, indicating the household may have been more affluent at one time but not anymore, as they had not been able to fix them. The seam on the leather was broken in a few places, so he worked on replacing the gut stitches and then reinforced the heels with additional thonging. Before he was done, he joined the girl in drinking more of the ale. They left the lean-to nearly an hour later, the newly mended shoes piled next to the empty barrel tipped on its side.

The image of Mousie's wide derriere sticking out of the barrel, her head deep inside, brought a smile to his face. He whistled for his broom, which teetered over to him, and they lifted into the night.

The next settlement was a *ráth* surrounded by a timber wall enclosing several roundhouses, workshops, and pathways, but the ropes lashing the tree trunks together needed repairing. Some of the trunks sagged, creating small gaps for intruders and wildlife.

As Lugh landed next to the wooden enclosure, the back tip of the broom bumped along the ground. Mousie giggled and nearly fell off.

"Quiet, you awful creature!"

This made her giggle harder as her arms tightened around him. "If I'm awful, then what are you?"

He almost smiled. How did she bring such joy to him?

He jabbed an elbow back, knocking her off the broom.

In the dark, it was hard to see her face as he brought the broom to a stop, but he imagined she looked stunned in her silence, and he grinned. Then she flung herself back on the still grass, spreading her arms out and breathing deep of the cool air. She hiccupped.

With a shake of his head, he approached the sagging palisade and wiggled his fingers. For a moment, his beard shimmered. The cut tree trunks groaned in their post holes, straightening along the line, the ropes squeaking as they tightened. Some of the rope he reinforced with new strands. When it was done, he held still, listening for any movement from the occupants of the *ráth*.

"Stupid people. Not even a guard."

Somebody should have awoken with all the noise. What if they had been under attack?

Stomping his little feet, he marched through the leather door flap of a roundhouse, finding only scraps for shoes. With quick work, he replaced some of the leather, reinforced other pieces, added stronger stitching, and in one case, added a little circle design on the top of a delicate pair of shoes lying next to a sleeping girl of maybe five or six years. He hoped the circle would remind her of the sun.

He also withdrew some of his newly made candles and set these next to the shoes.

Mousie followed him wherever he went, silent in her padded footsteps. A tickle marched up his back, and he glanced at her. In the dark, her light-colored eyes seemed intent in their watchfulness. Heat burned his cheeks, so he turned his back to her, ignoring her once more.

They didn't stay long enough in this poor homestead to drink their ale even if they had enough for themselves. Instead, Lugh yanked Mousie back onto the broom, and they zoomed above the fixed walls. Quickly, he eyed the palisade for any holes, but satisfied with his work, he left.

The broom whipped through the night at a dizzying speed. The girl braced herself against him, her fingers locking together around his waist, and he felt warmth in his cheeks again.

Then the broom slowed, hovering over a newly constructed *ráth*. A stone palisade, numerous penned sheep and pigs, two dozen or more cattle, and well-cared-for roundhouses. He sniffed. A wealthy establishment. He urged the broom away. Not more than a quarter of an hour further on, they came to another settlement. This one needed help.

Like the last homestead they had visited, he mended everything he found broken and fixed all the household's shoes, leaving behind new candles. Mousie followed him silently, helping where her mortal hands could offer assistance. The work was time-consuming, and he got thirsty. After finishing his tasks, he guided the broom back to the previous wealthy *ráth*.

He bypassed all the roundhouses, heading straight for their storage lean-to. Before stepping through the wall, he flicked Mousie's ear.

She squeaked and covered the injured ear. "What was that for?"

Because he hated her. "Follow me, cabbage head."

He ignored her frown as he stepped inside and found a block of wood to pull close to the first barrel. He swallowed several ladlefuls of ale. The tight ball in the pit of his stomach loosened.

Feeling generous, he offered the ladle to Mousie.

When the liquid was too far out of reach inside the barrel, they slid against the wooden sides. He patted his belly, his head swimming. Mousie hiccupped next to him. It was nice to feel her warm shoulder against his. For a few moments, he floated in those surprising emotions.

Then he shoved her away as he climbed to his feet.

From his bag, he withdrew a mallet, the perfect size for his small hands and stature. Mousie stared up at him with shining eyes, her mouth turned down in a pout. He swung his arms back, then slammed the mallet into the barrel above her head.

Like a pig, she squealed as ale burst forward and sloshed all over her. He laughed aloud. When she tried to scramble to her feet, and her hands slipped on the muddy ground, he bent over double, tears streaming down his cheeks.

When the laughter subsided, he wiped his eyes.

Mousie put plump hands on her hips. Ale and mud darkened her beard and hair. Her eyes squinted to slits. "Do you have no respect at all for others?"

"Why should I?"

She huffed. "Don't you want to be treated well?"

"Most everybody I know don't deserve to be alive, let alone be coddled."

She shook one of her feet, kicking free a clump of mud. "You fix people's shoes." She wrung out her beard, casting a surreptitious glance his way. "I think there's a good man hiding underneath that rough exterior."

"What would you know, Mousie?"

Jerking mud off her hands, she stepped close to him. He jolted back, blinking rapidly as she took one of his hands. Even with man hands, her fingers were delicate as they traced the lines on his thumb.

She glanced up at him through her lashes. "I know you have a dog that you love and miss. You've let me keep the eagle even though I'm sure he reminds you of your beloved hound." She dropped his hand, and he felt lost in that second of her retreat. "I know that even though you have been mad at me, yelled at me, you have given me everything I need to survive."

He saw fear lurking in her eyes, as if she might not believe her own words, but she straightened her shoulders.

Then the insipid girl twirled around, her head tilted to look up at the top of the lean-to. She breathed deep before continuing. "I know that you creep into people's houses at night and fix their shoes, but you only visit a rich man's house to drink his ale." She stilled, facing him again. Her arms hugged herself. "These things about you tell me everything I need to know that you are a good man."

He froze, his mouth gaping open, the very breath caught in his throat as it sought to escape. When was the last time anyone had belief in him? Now this silly mouse of a girl gave him more credit than he deserved. Because really, he didn't deserve nice words.

He closed his mouth.

He couldn't allow this simple creature to affect him. A different type of heat made his cheeks hot. He ground his teeth together. "Nonsense conjecture."

In a smooth movement, he whipped out the Druid rod and touched it to her nose. The small reddish-brown mouse replaced the leprechaun man-woman. He scooped her up and dropped her into his jacket pocket.

CHAPTER 13

LILY SMASHED HER LIPS CLOSED.

Everything about the centaurs' home, including the centaurs themselves, surprised and amazed her. Both parents were extremely accommodating, not at all surprised at the strays their son brought home. With open smiles, they had brought them all inside, even the bear.

The four-sided house had polished poles set in two parallel rows. Each wooden pole had an additional pole lashed tightly near the top to extend the roof higher—enough clearance for the centaurs' taller statures. Familiar wickerwork filled in the walls between the poles, with the outsides plastered over with lime. Two more rows of poles marched down the center of the home, supporting the straw-covered roof. A central hearth provided warmth, smoke billowing around the huge stew pot and leaving out through a hole above it.

Lily sniffed where she sat near the fire on a mat of woven reeds. The stew didn't smell like anything she had ever eaten before. She hid pursed lips behind her hand. No need to offend anyone.

But Sophronia—the female centaur—caught her sniff. Her chestnut coloring nearly matched her son's coat with an additional tint of red, but she swept back long, flaxen hair. The length extended fully down her back and spread out over her withers. Her creamy midriff was bare, a too-short grass-woven blouse barely covering her breasts. The neckline dipped into a deep V-shape, accentuating her bosom.

White patches circled her doe eyes, while she stirred the evening meal and responded to Lily's reaction. "Oats and grass, boiled with delicate watercress with a handful of other herbs and spices."

Lily crossed her arms over her raised knees and tried ever so slowly to

66

cover her nose. The meal stunk worse than a three-day-dead possum sitting under a full summer sun.

Fintan sat to her left, concentrating on the cauldron with one eye. "Do you add any meat to that stew of yours?"

Sophronia gasped, her hands close to her chest. "Never!" Her eyes widened. "We cannot find it in ourselves to eat our brother and sister creatures."

"Blasphemous," Fintan said under his breath. He tapped his legs in time to the young centaur who played his wooden pipes while he skipped circles around the room on his horses' legs.

Once, Lily had wondered about eating the very animals she spoke to. When her and her sisters were all younger, they had made a pact never again to eat animals from land, air, or sea. That left crickets, ants, and spiders. That hadn't been appetizing at all, so they quickly went back to eating the creatures they'd shunned.

On her other side, the bear laid on his belly. She stroked one of his outstretched paws while watching the family scene unfold. The aromatic scent of hay, grass, and oats, which lined the floors, lingered in the air, barely masking the awful smell of the stew.

The boy's father beat his chest in time to the music and laughed aloud. A moment later, he added a few lyrics. Like his son, Astylos the centaur was naked above the waist, firelight tripping along his heavily muscled shoulders and chest. His own long, dark hair curled down his back and over his brown coat.

Everyone cheered when the song ended.

Daric's cheeks brightened red as he knelt next to the bear. He was out of breath as he spoke. "Is the meal done yet, Mother?"

Sophronia smiled down at him, her brown eyes softening. "Almost, my dear colt."

The boy nodded, then pet the bear, who released a rumble of pleasure. "What's his name?"

Lily touched a finger to her parted lips. She had never thought to call the animal anything. Her lamb back home was just lamb. The bear was just bear.

She reached out to the creature to increase her connection with him and sent a message. She linked herself to the flower she was named for, then spoke to him. "What's your name?"

The bear responded enthusiastically, raising his head as he flashed images at her, but it was tricky since he couldn't use words. She saw fuzzy human feet clad in a warrior's heavy-soled boots, which seemed familiar to her. Next was the image of a man's fist opening one finger at a time until the palm splayed out. That image repeated several times, flashing five fingers at her.

"Cúig?" she said in a whisper. It meant five.

With a too-human sigh, the bear plopped his head back down on his crossed paws.

Perhaps not the right name, but it would do for now. She leaned against Cúig, rubbing his ear, smelling deep of his musky scent. He closed his eyes, dreamy images reaching her. They were mostly of berries.

Daric jumped to his hooves, clomping over to a wall where numerous musical instruments hung. He stowed away the pipes and brought down a harp. He plucked a few strings, and the music washed over Lily. She closed her eyes, moved by the sound. To her, no instrument sounded as melodic as the harp, if played correctly.

The chords stopped.

"Do you play?"

Her eyes popped open, the young centaur's stare intense on her. His fingers hung in the air above the strings.

She nodded.

Ambling over to her, he leaned down to hand her the harp before sitting back.

The smooth wood fit warmly in her hands. Experimentally, she plucked the chords to check their tuning as she sat up. It sounded perfect. Her fingers moved more assuredly across the strings, plucking the melody that had haunted her since Marigold had died.

Music filled the room, a sadness tinging the end of each chord. The centaurs each kneeled to the ground, all eyes on her, but she blocked them out as she closed her eyes, allowing the music to infuse her very soul.

Then the words came, her voice surer than it had been since her sister's death.

Soft winds sighed across the sea
the day we played in clear waters.
Then a wave bent your knee
and Mum lost one of her daughters.
I sorrowed to leave you
where the ocean meets the sky,
but the wide sea I could not swim over
and neither had I wings to fly.
Autumn fades your memory,
and every day I wallow in sadness.
The birds keep singing in the tree
but my grief will not vanish.
The ocean's salty breath haunts me,

while I here sit all alone and cold,
seeing us as three beautiful flowers,
but we've lost our Marigold.
We've lost our Marigold.
I weep and weep,
because we've lost our Marigold.

She played a few more chords after the last line, the music trilling at the end and reverberating in its final notes.

She opened her eyes to applause. At first, she couldn't see because tears clouded her vision. She flicked them away hurriedly. The bear nuzzled her side, and she buried her face in his fur, grateful for his warmth.

When her breath stabilized, she faced the room. Sophronia clasped her hands over her breasts and tears streaked down her long face. Daric's father, Astylos, coughed a couple of times, while the young centaur pushed to his hooves once more and came to her side. He kneeled there, reaching for the harp, which she happily surrendered.

"I've never lost anyone, but I can imagine the pain. I felt it as you played the music." His voice sounded so young and afraid. "Was that your sister?"

She nodded, retreating into her muteness.

He reached a thin arm out to place a hand on her shoulder. "Don't worry, we'll help you find your other sister."

CHAPTER 14

WITH THE BROOM IN HAND, Lugh leapt off the roof of the centaurs' home, dropping Mousie back into his pocket. He cleared away a tear once he was sure that the girl couldn't see him. Her sister's song echoed in his mind. He'd lost someone like that once, but he couldn't remember who.

He furrowed his brow. A large, black-browed man swam up from his memories, but just as he saw the comely man's gray eyes, the image was gone again.

The broom sped through the twilight night, then jolted to a stop when a black cloud coalesced in front of them. Lugh jerked away, lowering to the forest ground and hopping off the broom.

The black cloud floated to the earth before swirling into a funnel. Wind kicked at leaves and small bushes. When it died, a young woman in all black appeared.

"Mórrígan."

"Lugh!" She hissed through her rowanberry-red lips. "Get rid of the sister."

"Ugly, old hag, get off my back!"

The woman was unfazed. She smiled, her teeth white against the stain of her painted mouth. "This is not a favor for me. This is for the good of all the Tuatha Dé Danann."

He narrowed his eyes. "You aren't one of us."

Wait, did that mean he was a Tuatha Dé Danann? He rubbed his temple. He couldn't remember anymore.

However, his last statement affected her this time. She raised a hand, then stopped. A smile replaced her twisted grin as she dropped her arm. "I am more of the people than you are in this diminished state." She laughed, a sound rich and loud in the twilight forest. "Besides, I'm one of the most powerful of our people and have fought on your side for a millennium."

Her smile dropped as she leaned forward, her silky black hair tickling his nose. He slapped it away, but nearly lost her presence as darkness enveloped her body. The black mists sucked all the light around them. Then her voice echoed. "If you don't help me, the One God will take over Éire, and the Otherworld will be gone forever. Do you want that?"

He shrugged but hunkered down. "What do I care?" He glared at the mass of darkness. "I want my dog back."

"Forget the dog!" Her pale face appeared in the dark cloud, hovering and disembodied.

Lugh stamped at the ground. "He's my hound. Would you ever tell Fionn mac Cumhaill to forget any of his hounds?" A light entered his awareness. "Why don't you awaken Fionn and his Fianna? They'd take care of the prophets from the One God."

She shook her head. "They're likely to start a war."

With rare insight, something he hadn't felt in so long, not since he had been as powerful as a god himself, he said, "War is inevitable."

Mórrígan closed her eyes for a brief instant. "Hopefully not. That's why I need to keep the girls separated. If my plan works, we'll keep out this new religion without bloodshed. But if it becomes necessary, kill the girl."

He chuckled. "I knew you lived for blood."

"Don't listen to faery tales. You know me, if you'd only remember."

He rolled his shoulders back, as if shrugging a weight off. "The only thing I remember is that I should hate you, but I don't know why."

A disembodied hand appeared as she rubbed her temple. "Just do what I ask."

"Off with you, old biddy."

An eyebrow rose, but she just clucked at him. "Get rid of the sister or kill the girl." Before fading into nothing, her pale face and hand melted away, the darkness dissipating.

Snatching at his broom, he set it to home. It didn't take long to zip through the forest to reach his mountain. When he crossed the threshold of the glass door, he whipped Mousie out and touched the Druid rod to her. This time he allowed her to have her own form. He was too agitated to care about her.

He crooked a finger at her, and she obliged, following him through the halls of glass walls.

"Your name is Lugh?" Her words echoed along the hallway. Fear haunted her voice.

"Whist!" He scowled at her. "Not for your lips."

She cringed. At the opening of his cave, she veered off to the rock wall where her chains piled on the floor.

The eagle hopped over to her, and when she held out an arm, he leapt to it, gentle in his perch as he kept in flight as long as possible before gripping her forearm. Her light fingers played over the creature's chest as she crooned to him.

The whole scene irritated Lugh further. Perhaps he should just kill the girl now.

With a flick of his wrist, the chains snapped around her left ankle, nearly yanking Mousie off her feet. Instinctively, she pulled the eagle close to her body, even as his wings spread out. Her brows drew down in a sharp vee, and she turned her back on him.

He slapped his bag of tools to the ground and raised his hands toward her, ready to deliver the killing blow. A golden glow lit up his beard.

Then, something stopped him. A voice at the back of his memories.

The Morrígan wasn't to be trusted, so why should he kill on her command?

He'd choose when to kill the girl. Perhaps when she was done amusing him.

With a satisfied nod, he turned back to his bag, the golden light fading, then took the tools out and stacked them in their rightful places in one of the other rooms. When he came back to the cave entrance, Mousie sat cross-legged on the ground, holding out a lizard to the bird.

Where had she gotten the lizard?

Perhaps it had been in the cave. Who knew exactly how far the cave went? Decades ago, he had followed the cave past his hoard of gold and precious gems, spending nearly two hours in the winding paths. But it had been never ending, so he'd stopped exploring.

Without looking up, Mousie addressed him. "Why am I and my sister important to you, Lugh?"

"You're not. Just scum." Using a stick, he poked gaps in the flames leaping in his hearth. "Don't say my name."

The girl ignored him. "But that woman said we had to be separated." Her eyes flicked up to peer at him, fear tightening her face. Her voice came out small. "Or you're supposed to kill me. But why?"

He threw the stick into the fire, staring into the orange and red flames licking the wood. "I don't know what that stinky woman is trying to do. None of my business."

"Then why am I here, Lugh?"

He spun around, stalking toward her in slow strides. At first, she jerked but then held steady. He felt she should shrink away, but she continued to sit there, her back straight. When he neared her, the top of his head barely reached her shoulder. "Why should I care about you? You're nothing." Spit dribbled onto his lips. "The mud on my shoes."

Her lashes swept down, hiding her thoughts from him, before looking back up. Firelight danced in the blue depths of her eyes and darkened her lashes. Her beauty stunned him. How could such simple things from this despicable creature affect him so much?

Her voice was a whisper. "You should care."

He flicked his wrist and several strands of her red hair snapped taut, ripping.

"Ow!"

One red strand floated free, and he snatched it out of the air. He waved a hand and the various candles squatting in the cave snuffed out. Only the hearth's fire threw shadows around the room.

Mousie watched him, pale and wide-eyed.

He snorted. Let her think death came for her soon, because he didn't know when he would change his mind.

He stopped before the hearth fire and brought up the strand in his fist. He whispered an incantation into his tightened fingers. A soft glow encased his fist.

Mórrígan wanted him to get rid of Mousie's sister. Yet the sister wouldn't give up. And now she had the help of the centaurs. So, the only way to accomplish his next mission was to bring the sister to him. Then he could take care of her.

He kissed his fist and let the fire singe the hair up to where his fingers balled together. With that done, he clambered into his fur-lined pallet on the opposite rock wall from where Mousie was chained. He could see her vague outline. She sat there, quiet. As he laid down, he remembered that he hadn't given Mousie anything to sleep on.

His heart skipped a beat as he weighed his options and how they'd make him feel.

Then he remembered he didn't care.

Served her right anyway. She should keep her distance and thoughts to herself.

As he drifted in and out of sleep, his balled hand relaxed. The strand of her hair slipped between his fingers.

CHAPTER 15

LILY DIDN'T KNOW WHY, but they found the leprechaun's home quicker than she'd expected, especially considering they had previously spent most of a day looking for it with no luck, and today they'd found it in less than an hour. With Cúig the bear beside her smelling faintly of musky berries, and Fintan only a few paces behind, they followed Astylos the centaur up to the glass walls of the little man's home.

Her stomach was uneasy at the thought of the centaurs living so close to the tricky little leprechaun. *What if he kidnapped their young colt?*

Astylos turned to her, bending his human half down and grabbing her hand as his dark face lowered near hers. "I will leave you here, Lily the human. May you find your sister and return home with the quickness of a swallow."

Lily nodded while chewing her lip.

He brushed his lips to her cheek before departing with a quick gallop.

She looked to the glass home stuck in the mountainside. How could she prepare herself for what might lie ahead? Prepare for the worst? But that meant a world without Rose. That wasn't a future she could comprehend.

The bear turned his great head to her, sending her a questioning image of the three of them trying to open the glass entrance. She shrugged. She had never seen such a door before. A metal object stuck out from it about midway down. She imagined it was some mechanism to pop the door open.

Unaware of the mental images passing between Lily and Cúig, Fintan cleared his throat. "Won't get nowhere just standing here, and I don't think the leprechaun will welcome us in."

Lily held her breath, her body humming with readiness, her back stiff and her spear arm rigid. She swallowed rapidly. She was so close to Rose, now. This time she would get her sister back.

She'd draw blood, even a little man's blood, if it meant that she would have Rose home safely tonight.

She slapped her thigh, something she'd always done if it meant she'd have to fight, then threw back her shoulders and walked up to the door, her footsteps sure and quick. She gripped the round metal in her hands and jiggled it. The glass slid outward.

Silence met them inside.

Taking a steady breath, she inched down the glass hallway. Fintan followed, his footsteps a faint padding on the stone floor. However, Cúig's claws clicked as he lumbered forward. She looked back at him once, and his head seemed to hunker into his shoulders. But he couldn't stop the clicking, so he gingerly took each footstep, like a cat trying to walk on water.

Even though the walls were made of glass, each room they passed was packed with the leprechaun's belongings so that they could not often see over to the next room. Tall stacks of wooden crates also cast shadows farther inside so that the overall effect was encroaching darkness.

At the doorway to each room, Lily held up a hand so that she could peer inside for any sign of the small man or Rose. She only found junk in most cases, but some objects were so curious in nature that she wanted to pick them up and check them out. She forced herself to move on because none of it would help her find Rose.

Then she saw the room filled with weapons. Amid the dozens of spears, daggers, knives, and axes, she might find something to help her against the magical leprechaun. She entered, guard up, checking around every cranny with each slow step. She fingered the blade of a curved ax. The handle looked thick and heavy. Too much for her.

How did the small man use it?

Maybe it was a war trophy.

The bear followed her around the room, his mind sending a plethora of images. They all showed a man wielding each weapon as the bear passed them.

Perhaps Cúig wished he were a man.

A shimmering glint caught her eye.

There, in the center of the room, wooden crates piled around it, a harp stood upright on a marble pedestal. A musical instrument in a room of weapons?

The frame was made of oak, carved with a double-headed fish design, studded with jeweled eyes. It only had three strings: one silver, one gold, and one bronze. Then, suddenly, she recognized it. *Daur da Bláo*, the Oak of Two Blossoms, the famous harp of the Dagda, one of the supposedly powerful Tuatha Dé Danann. He was the All-Father of the mythical people, highly skilled and wise, associated with fertility, agriculture, life, and death.

Could the harp do what the legends suggested?

She tilted her head back, looking through the glass roof. Who had a glass house but a figure of legend? What land had an ocean for sky but a land of the Otherworld?

How did mythical creatures like the dragon and centaurs exist except in the land of the faery?

She brought her chin down. The stories her mother had told of the Otherworld were all real, and this was a magical harp, capable of much more than music.

She reached for it. Something fizzed in the air, pricking her skin with tiny jolts, but the moment her hands closed over the oak base, it stopped. The harp was hers, and she would use it if needed. Anything to get Rose back.

Spear in one hand, harp secured to her back harness, she continued the trek down the hallway, still pausing at each doorway, looking for danger before moving on. Lily was happy for the single hallway because they could quickly become lost, even with glass walls.

Then the sound of multiple voices made her pause. The disembodied voices continued, which meant they were not aware of her and the others. Ever so softly, she crept forward, motioning for the old man and the bear to stay back.

After another dozen paces, the ground became uneven as it inclined. Through the glass, Lily could make out wavering figures. She dropped to her belly, slid forward, hand by hand, until coming to a cavernous room at the end of the hallway.

She scanned the cave entrance. To the far right, Rose stood, one ankle chained to the wall. Her sister held a hand to her mouth while focusing on the other two figures in the room. Lily followed her line of sight. One was the little man, his profile to her, and he seemed to be in a heated conversation with the other person, a woman garbed in a tightly fitted black dress that trailed on the ground. Various parts of the clothing vanished, leaving the woman partly nude until the material reappeared.

"Fool! You thought bringing the other sister here was the way to get rid of her?"

The little man knew Lily would come to him? Her hands turned clammy, her heartbeat racing. Every breath sounded loud in her ears.

Was this a trap?

Lily slowed down her breath as her heart raced, then peered more closely at the strange woman. Something about her was familiar. She was as pale as lime with long, black hair. Not someone Lily had ever seen before, but the curve of her cheeks and nose sparked her memory.

The little man spat at the ground in front of the woman. "You told me to get rid of her. So, I'm doing it my way."

The woman's pale fingers pinched the bridge of her nose. "It's dangerous to have them so close to each other here."

"What would you have me do, hag of crows?"

She pointed to Rose. "I will kill the girl now."

Lily surged to her feet, her yell echoing in the cave. "No!"

She threw her spear toward the black-clad woman just as both the little man and the woman spun toward her. The strange woman flicked her wrist at the same time and the spear went through black smoke to clatter in the darkness beyond the cave's opening.

The little man narrowed his eyes on Lily. "Hallo, thief."

Lily bit her lip. He must have seen the harp on her back. When she reached for the instrument, his eyebrows arched on his lined face.

"I'll kill you, you filthy poacher, before you can use that harp."

Not knowing what the man could actually do, she stopped. She allowed her gaze to flicker toward Rose for a second. Her sister chewed her thumb, blue eyes wide with fear. Lily's body hummed with energy, ready to fight and kill to save Rose, and she slid small steps toward her, her knuckles turning white as she wished for her spear back. "Give me my sister."

He snorted. "And what do you think you can do if I don't, spineless creature?"

Her hands fisted tighter. *Had I thought it would be as easy as asking for Rose?*

No. That was why she took the harp, which remained useless strapped to her back.

Cúig and Fintan's entrance into the room gave Lily the distraction she needed to edge even closer to her Rose. She bent down to test the chains. An eagle hopped over to her. The same that had gone through the portal when the leprechaun had taken Rose.

Meanwhile, Fintan hobbled forward with his walking stick. "Lugh, come home. Your sister is worried about..."

The little man waved his hand, and Fintan disappeared in a flash of blinding light.

Lily rocked back on her heels, dropping the chains. *Did he kill the old man?*

The old man who had named the leprechaun.

She frowned. *Did Fintan know the leprechaun then? What if his knowledge could have helped her get Rose back?*

She grunted in frustration. *Too late.* And too late for the old man.

She tamped down her anger as Cúig suddenly surged forward. The eagle took a big leap at the same time. Again, the small man waved his hand, and the bear vanished in light. The eagle screeched and skidded to a stop on the rocky ground.

Lily felt a tear rip through her heart, hammering against her chest.

Not Cúig! Why had she allowed the bear to come along?

When the leprechaun faced her, she held herself very still in a crouched position. Cold beads of fear tripped down her spine. She didn't want to die. She didn't want Rose to die.

The little man's beady eyes looked her up and down. "What do you plan to do, nigmenog?"

Summoning her courage, Lily answered him, her voice cracking. "I would like my sister back."

He rubbed his beard, his fingers going all the way to the shorn ends. "Foolish flower."

She slapped her thigh, releasing energy, prepared for a final stand. "Release my sister."

The little man raised his hands.

"Lugh, no." Rose latched onto Lily's shoulder, pulling her back, ready to share her fate if the leprechaun killed her. She gave Lily a look, one that said Lily should understand something else was happening here, but Lily couldn't fathom it now.

Instead, she marveled at her sister, who was ready to sacrifice her life. Then Lily thought of something. She quickly held up a palm to the little man. "What if we could do a trade?"

He halted in his movements, his bushy eyebrows quirking. "A trade?"

Lily reached inside the hidden pocket sewn into her tunic and withdrew the coin the beautiful woman named Hera had given her. "This is solid gold." She wasn't sure that was the truth but said it anyway. The little man seemed to like treasure. "I will trade you this coin for Rose."

The side of his mouth twitched, as if considering the proposition, but then frowned. "Not good enough. I'll keep Mousie." His hands rose again.

Her chest seized in a panic. "Wait!" Again, he halted at her hoarse request. "What can I do?"

Rose linked her hand with Lily's. "Please, Lugh," she said, her tone husky.

The little man looked with surprise at Rose, then his eyes narrowed. He scratched his chin and looked up out of the corner of his eye. Then his whole face lit up. "Find my hound."

"Your dog?"

"Yes. Find Failinis, and I swear by the sun to release your sister to you."

Lily frowned. "But I wouldn't know how or where to start."

He flicked his hands at her in a shooing motion. "Out with you, feckless vermin. You'll find my horse, Enbarr, beyond the door of my mountain home. She will take you back to your land, where I lost my hound. When you have found him, only then will Enbarr bring you back." He touched a finger to his bulbous nose. "However, the horse will return on her own in one week's time. If you haven't found my beloved Failinis by then, you will never be able to return."

Uneasy with having to leave her sister, Lily was also relieved to have found a way to save her without either of them dying. She released Rose's hand. "I'll be back," she whispered.

Wrinkling her brow, Rose looked worried, and Lily almost couldn't walk away. Then she smiled, which gave Lily the encouragement needed to purposefully leave her sister in captivity with an uncertain future. But now there was hope that Rose could be freed.

She pocketed the coin and turned.

"You'll return my harp when you bring me my dog!" His voice carried down the glass hallway. "Foul bandit."

Then she ran. A part of her wanted to cry in frustration, but a large part of her was determined. She'd find the little man's dog, and then she would bring Rose safely home. She might even use the harp on him just for taking her sister.

If she didn't die first for trying.

CHAPTER 16

BACK OUTSIDE, THE BRIGHT SUN seared Lily's skin. She glanced up at the ocean above, hearing the crash of violent waves.

Please Mother Goddess, keep Rose safe.

Nothing could be done for Fintan or Cúig. She squeezed back tears and looked around for the leprechaun's horse.

Grazing along the tree line that led back into the dense yew forest, Enbarr, a pure white horse, seemed unaware of her.

Lily blinked in surprise. The horse hadn't been there before.

Would Enbarr take her back through the well? She wasn't sure they could fit, but she'd find out soon enough. With calm, steady steps, she cautiously approached. The mare's big brown eyes glanced at her, as she munched at the grass. She didn't shy away when Lily laid a hand on the warm flesh of her neck. The flowing white mane was silky beneath her fingers.

Lily had never been on a horse before. The warriors at *Dún Neidín* ran and vaulted onto their mounts, but she was sure she couldn't do the same without practice. How would she get on?

Tentatively, she sent a message to the animal, stating her intention.

Enbarr bent a front knee, bringing her back down a bit. Then she bent her other front knee, followed by the back legs. Last, she rose into a sitting position while showing Lily an image.

Lily knew this was her cue to climb aboard. As the horse pushed up her back legs, Lily clasped the strong neck. A sweet scent rose from the soft mane and filled her nose.

Soon the horse broke into a canter. Lily bounced around at first, nearly falling off, until she finally relaxed and let her body move in time with the horse's, finding her center of gravity. Then they flew through the forest like the winter winds in a snowstorm.

For most of the run, Lily kept her eyes closed, thinking they'd crash into a tree at the speeds they traveled. After what seemed like mere minutes, they emerged from the forest, back under the scorching sun and onto sloping plains.

Enbarr slowed to a gait as she climbed the long hill up to the well. As she neared, she leapt straight at it. Lily gasped and slammed her eyes shut, tightening her arms around the horse's neck.

Surely, they would collide with the small opening!

Instead, water encased her, and she struggled for a breath, but this lasted only an instant as they reemerged on the other side. Enbarr stilled.

Lily opened her eyes, wiping water from her face. Frigid wind slapped her cheeks. Her breath hung in the air. It was much cooler than before. The sun winked a final goodbye in the horizon amid a splash of pinks and oranges.

They were back by the well in Éire.

She pat Enbarr's neck and marveled at the horse's dry coat. How had the horse avoided being soaked? Smoothing back wet strands of her own blonde hair, Lily relayed a message to the horse.

The direction for home.

Again, the horse took off at a quick run. Didn't she ever tire? Perhaps not, considering she was a supernatural creature.

The journey to *Ráth Bláthanna* lasted less than half an hour, the sky darkening and a full moon rising in the northeast. As they drew near the wooden palisade, she sent a message to halt, not willing to risk an attack if the sentry didn't recognize her atop the all-white horse. And why would they? No one owned horses at their settlement, so seeing her on such a magnificent creature would be a surprise.

Odhran, the older of the Winkle brothers, popped up over the top of the gate. "I see you, Líle níc Muaich." His eyes grew wide at the sight of the horse. In his eleven years of life, he'd probably only seen a couple of horses, and none so magnificent as Enbarr.

"I see you, Odhran mac Domangairt."

If possible, his eyes widened even more at her response, such simple words but more than what people had heard her utter since Marigold's death. Odhran waited expectantly for more, perhaps hoping for an explanation about the horse, but she remained quiet, so he shrugged and disappeared. The gate groaned open moments later.

When she entered, she looked around for the visitors who might have stayed an extra night for the Samhain celebration. But while the hard ground captured dozens of footsteps crossing over each other, the *ráth* now lay quiet. No sleeping bodies surrounded the central fire, so the visitors must have gone home. And with nightfall, the livestock would have already been brought in and the evening meal done.

Her stomach growled.

It may have been early morning when she left the Otherworld, but she hadn't eaten anything since the prior evening. Sophronia the centaur had offered bread of ground straw and hay before she'd headed out to find the leprechaun's home, but the bread hadn't appealed to her.

Odhran now descended the stone rampart to meet her, gazing wonderingly up at Enbarr. His youthful voice pitched high. "Glad to see you back! It's been nearly a week since you left."

A week? But it had only been two days. Then she remembered that Fintan had said time moved differently.

The boy looked past her. "Rose didn't make it back?"

Lily shook her head at him before looking to either side of the horse, thinking of how to get down. She finally decided to bring one leg over and slide down to the ground.

Odhran reached a tentative hand up, his fingers mere inches from Enbarr's nose. "Can I touch her?"

She gestured to the horse, so the boy gleefully stroked her. The majestic animal allowed the pet before shaking out her mane, then she circled about and galloped outside the *ráth*. She stopped just beyond the walls and looked for suitable grass in the field.

"Guess she don't want to be cooped up in here," Odhran said.

Lily stared after the horse, thoughts running through her mind. The little man had said she could keep Enbarr until she found his dog, but would the horse allow that? The creature had a mind of her own. With a full moon shining down on her, Enbarr seemed even more magical, glittering in the moonlight.

She breathed deeply to settle a tremor starting in the pit of her belly. It would be what it would be. She turned on her heel to make her way to her family's roundhouse. Her lips trembled and her hands shook with each heavy footstep.

She would have to face mamaí with another daughter lost.

The breath caught in the back of her throat as she forced back a shudder.

Odhran must have spread the word that she was back already before she had even entered the *ráth*. She barely made it within a dozen paces of her family's warm home when her mother met her outside. Shadows drew long lines across Ciara's face, her eyes dark and hooded. She stared at her daughter for a full second before opening her arms. Lily fell into them, bending her head down to her mother's breast. Tears stung her eyes, but she refused to allow them to fall.

A rumbling growl jerked her away from Ciara, and she gasped with surprise. Happiness filled her at seeing her friend and companion, the bear. Cúig stayed on all fours as he nuzzled his head against her side, rubbing his musky scent on her. She wrapped her arms around his neck, sending him a wave of images to express her joy at finding him safe. He returned the same thoughts.

Ciara chuckled at their affectionate display. "I'm glad for your return."

Lily lost her smile as she straightened and looked at her mother. "The leprechaun took Rose."

Her mother nodded her head toward the roundhouse. "Fintan told us."

Eyebrows raised, Lily was surprised yet again. She had been sure that the leprechaun had killed her friends. She looked past her mother to see the old man nearly all in shadow against the roundhouse. At first, Lily pressed a palm against her heart, relieved that Fintan had been spared as well.

Then she remembered that the old man had known the leprechaun and had even called him by name. Lugh. The same that Rose had used.

Her nostrils flared. All the sadness, all the disappointment, all the guilt she felt in having lost Rose built into something hot, churning in her very core. She stepped past her mother and bored a finger into the old man's chest.

He didn't flinch. Instead, his one good eye measured her. His lips thinned, then he nodded. "I should have told ye that I knew who we were looking for."

Lily balled her fists. The bear padded next to her and nuzzled her fist to soothe her. She blew out the breath she had been holding, then dropped down to her knees to throw her arms around Cúig again. He was a loyal friend. His presence reassured her in so many ways. A warm acceptance she hadn't felt in such a long time.

She hid her face in his black fur, willing back her frustrations. Then she stood to face her mother. How much had Fintan told her? The last time she had seen Ciara, both she and Rose had left to find the missing Greek soldier.

The Greek soldier.

She rubbed her temple. In all the events of the past two days, she had forgotten about him. Hopefully he had survived the cold nights. There was nothing she could do for him now. But a thought took shape. She could continue the original mission.

"I must go speak with Mug Ruith." Her voice croaked with so many words spoken over the last two days.

Her diminutive mother grasped Lily's hands. Her dark brows first arched, then they bowed lower, the corners of her mouth drooping.

"Why?"

Lily glanced at the old man.

"I told her the leprechaun had taken your sister and then we had found her. That's all I knew to tell her."

She nodded and looked down at her mother. At least she didn't have to tell her that Rose was dead. "I can get Rose back, but I must find the leprechaun's dog."

Fintan blew out a huff.

But it was Ana who suddenly appeared from the roundhouse to intrude on the conversation. "That's an impossible task. How would you even know where to look?"

Ciara turned her face up to the *bandraoi*, and the two women linked hands. Their love for each other assured Lily that some things were still right in the world. Moonlight slanted over their faces, and something tickled at the back of Lily's memory. She shook her head. Too many fancies. Perhaps a product of her magic-filled days.

She cleared her throat, her voice hoarse. "The *Ard-Draoi* can help." She looked between her mother and Fintan, then settled on Ana. "Unless you know a way to find the hound."

Ana sighed and reached out a hand to cup Lily's cheek. "I'm sorry, my love, but my magic is not strong enough for that. But the High Druid? Too dangerous. He'll want something in return."

Lily straightened her back. She would do whatever she had to in order to save Rose from the leprechaun and bring her home. She would make sure Rose stayed alive.

She met the eyes of the three people and the bear studying her. Fintan nodded at what he saw there in her. Cúig brushed against her side. Her mother's lower lip trembled, and tears shined in her eyes.

Ana sighed, crossing her arms over her bosom. "I suppose you're resigned then."

Lily gave one short nod.

CHAPTER 17

SINCE THE SUN HAD SET and Lily needed real food, they waited several hours to make the journey toward the *Ard-Draoi*'s home. She planned to leave as soon as possible. While soaking up venison stew with a real piece of bread, Lily used the time to share everything that had happened with her mother and Ana.

The words poured out. More words than all the combined words she had spoken since Marigold's death.

They also talked about Marigold. All the emotions that had been kept close to her heart burst from her lips like water from a broken dam. Try as she might to keep some of it back, it emptied until there was nothing left to say.

Ana and Ciara flanked her on either side and all through her outpouring of grief, shame, and hurt, they hugged her. This brought new tears to her eyes, which she quickly dashed away.

Cúig made his way in during the night, plopping down with a heavy thud and curling against her back, the scent of berries wafting over her. Then he began to snore. She chuckled and rubbed a hand down his fur, but it didn't disturb him.

Abruptly, the bleak weight of her mission loomed inside, causing her chest to tighten. "What if I fail Rose?" she asked her mother. *What if the leprechaun kills her?*

Ciara shook her head. "You won't."

But she'd failed once already.

Ciara brought Lily's head to her lap, her fingers brushing through her fine, white hair, and Lily snuggled into her mother's warmth. She used to do this as a little girl, and it had always soothed her. She wished she could go back to being that little girl. A time when all her sisters had been alive and safe. A time when Ana had helped them learn how to use their special gifts. A time when the world was a magical place filled with a forest full of new animals she could talk to.

She was no longer that naïve girl.

What if her mother was wrong about her failing?

She spoke her fears aloud. Everything that could go wrong on her trip to *Oileán Dairbhre*, the meeting with the *Ard-Draoi* himself, the journey to find the missing hound, and then facing the leprechaun should she succeed in finding Failinis.

Ciara's fingers halted on her hair, and Lily sat up. "The gods are on your side. Through perseverance, you will succeed."

Ana took her hand from her other side and squeezed it. "But we'll love you even if you can't free Rose."

"Yes." Ciara's voice was low, the sound of tears at the end of the word. "I will always love you, Lily. No matter what happens, because I know the love you have for your sister and your family. I know you will never give up. That love will save us all, even if our family is broken apart."

Lily closed her eyes and sighed. Neither her mother nor Ana would stop loving her if she failed. She had probably known that…but would she stop loving herself?

As they continued talking, recalling happier times, Nana woke up and listened while she packed Lily's satchel with the supplies she would need for the full-day walk.

When the sun still had a few hours before dawn and there were no words left to say, Lily stood and scrubbed her face. Her throat felt raw. "Mamaí, Nana, I promise to bring Rose home." *Or die trying.*

Her grandmother clasped her hands together over one of Lily's. "We know you will, child."

Ciara took Lily's hand next when Nana released her and interlaced Lily's fingers with her own. "Do what you can, Lily. May the Great Goddess Danu look after you and your sister." Ciara squeezed her hand before turning to Ana. Her mother's eyes softened at the edges and her lips parted. "My darling…" No other words made it past the choke in her throat, and the two women embraced.

Lily looked down at her feet as her mother kissed her lifelong partner. She was grateful that Ana had chosen to accompany her but knew her mother would miss Ana as she did every time the *bandraoi* left to administer to other settlements. Ciara needed to stay behind for Nana, which Lily understood. However, since Ana was a *bandraoi*, the *Ard-Draoi* may take Lily's request more seriously.

Cúig shook his shaggy head and yawned wide with a small roar before lumbering to his feet. Lily used the cue to accept the leather satchel from her grandmother, kissing her on the cheek. She strapped the *Daur da Bláo*, the Dagda's magical harp, and a spare spear to her harness. Not knowing what else to say after that, having said so much in the last few hours, she nodded one last time and ducked outside.

The cold air slapped her awake. She should have slept but knew that she would have only tossed under the furs. The frosty wind would reinforce her drive to reach her sister as soon as possible.

Fintan already waited for her, leaning against the lime-plastered wall of the roundhouse, his frayed cloak pulled over his bald head. The old man still desired a way to the leprechaun's home but had yet to fully explain his relationship with the small man.

Lily would find out why.

With Fintan, Ana, and Cúig, Lily departed the *ráth* with little fanfare. Besides Rose, she knew the best and fastest route through the mountains to reach the northern shores.

A lump stuck in her throat at the thought of her sister.

The *Ard-Draoi* had to help her find Lugh's hound.

Outside the palisade, she found Enbarr alert, but let the horse walk with her in the lead instead of riding. Her thighs were still tender from last evening's ride.

The beginning of their travels started fairly level after they came off the hill of their settlement. Lily guided them southwest at first, striking a path through *An Caorthann Coill* to miss the rising elevations, but far enough north of *Dún Neidín* and the other smaller settlements along *An Abhainn As Ceann Mhara*, the River at the Head of the Sea.

When the sun rose, it was a welcome warmth. Surprisingly, the sun's strength was enough to chase away most of the mist lingering along the forest floor. Then the trees thinned as small rolling hills rose out of the ground. Broken slabs of rock and standing stones dotted the landscape more frequently. Soon they'd be crowded by mountains.

At midmorning, they came to *Bealach Béime*, Pass of the Notch. The rocky and uneven pass slithered through two extremely sloped mountains in a "V," creating the notch. The steep mountain sides glowed with golden gorse bushes, which wafted their sweet, exotic vanilla smell down toward the visitors.

Lily signaled a break.

Her back groaned as she dropped her satchel to the ground, then she dropped herself to the rocky path and leaned against Cúig's side where he laid, head resting on crossed front paws. She offered a strip of dried bacon, and the bear opened his mouth to accept it without shifting his head.

Ana drank from her waterskin, stretching afterward while Fintan sat atop a boulder not far away. He looked weary, and Lily thought she should be worried. She wanted to offer Enbarr for him to ride, but then she remembered that he had withheld information the first time they had traveled together.

Perhaps he would be more forthcoming this time. "What else should we know about Lugh?" Her voice cracked and she rubbed her throat.

He adjusted his eyepatch before responding. "Lugh is not what he seems. That leprechaun you see is not really him."

"Lugh is not a leprechaun?"

Fintan scratched his jutted chin. "Well, he is, and he is not."

"That is not very clear." She pinched her lips together.

"Stop confusing the girl." Ana exhaled sharply, pulling a loose thread from the tan tunic under her brown dress.

Fintan shot the *bandraoi* a dark look. "Lugh is the original leprechaun, but he didn't start life that way..."

Like the iron spearhead fitting into the right piece of grooved wood, it all locked into place for Lily. "Lugh the leprechaun is really Lugh Lámfada, Lugh of the Long Arm. The demigod accepted as one of the Tuatha Dé Danann." That was why Rose seemed to emphasize his name when Lily had tried to rescue her.

Fintan snapped his fingers. "You got it! He is a leprechaun, but he shouldn't be."

"And he can change back to the way he was before?"

The old man shrugged. "My wife thinks so, but no one knows how."

Lily rested her chin in her hands. "Why did he change?"

Ana waved her hand to dismiss Fintan's response. "When the Tuatha Dé Danann were banished to the Otherworld, many of them grew less in stature."

Fintan drummed fingers on his walking stick, humming in acquiescence. "This is one theory. Another is that he hasn't been the same since his son, Cúchulainn, died, and this may have caused him to diminish in his form."

Ana nodded. "Yes, there's a strange magic invading the Otherworld lands. It changes those who have much to regret."

Lily tilted her head in thought. "Does that mean all leprechauns are gods?"

"Some," Fintan said. "But Lugh has also transformed others, like mortals, into leprechauns so that he wouldn't be alone. Funny thing is that leprechauns are mean loners. He can be a nasty creature. They can't stand other people or even each other."

He chuckled at his words, but Lily felt dread in her middle. If Lugh couldn't stand Rose anymore, would he kill her, even as Lily still searched for or even found his hound?

Fintan tapped his staff on the ground. "I think some leprechauns have been changed by others who thought the creature was funny-looking. All of it doesn't really matter, anyhow. My wife will not leave me alone about trying to make him remember himself. That's his sister, you see."

Ana ran fingers through her long, chestnut-brown hair, releasing snags. "I wouldn't get involved." She traveled a little way up the path to peer around the first curve, then turned back. "Some gods are better off not remembering what their powers are."

Fintan frowned. "Lugh always used his powers for the good of the people. As the Sun God, he has brought enlightenment to others. He was even made one of the Tuatha Dé Danann when he led them in a winning war against their oppressors, the Fomorians."

Ana perched on a taller boulder across from Fintan. "Bah, the Morrígan had more to do with the wars than Lugh, helping the Tuatha Dé Danann defeat the Firbolgs first. In fact, Lugh finished planning for the Battle of Magh Tuireadh by seeking counsel from the Morrígan. She is the goddess of war and death, after all."

The two stared at each other with hard gazes, Ana leaning forward.

Lily climbed to her feet, signaling that it was time to restart their walk, giving a good reason for the conversation to end. Fintan strained so much coming to his feet, even with his walking stick, that she could no longer bear not to help him.

"Ride Enbarr." She said it in such a way that she expected no argument, so Fintan nodded.

When he was safely secured and Enbarr back on her feet, the old man sighed. "How long until we reach the High Druid?"

Lily glanced up at him as she led the way. "If we do not stop too long at the next break, we'll reach the north shore settlement at *An Caladh* an hour after moonrise." From there, they would have to cross to *Oileán Dairbhre*, the island home of the *Ard-Draoi*.

Although she had seen the shores of the High Druid's island from *An Caladh*, the Rest Place by the Sea, she had never crossed the channel, nor had she ever known anyone else to seek out the High Druid. Her stomach fluttered, but she quickly tamped it down. Like she had said before, she would do whatever the *Ard-Draoi* asked of her.

As they traversed the narrow pass, Lily remembered what Fintan had said about Lugh the leprechaun the first time they had met. "What did the leprechaun take from you?"

Fintan gave a wiry smile while straightening his eye patch. "My peace."

CHAPTER 18

AT MIDDAY, THEY REACHED a turning point in their journey, where the pass widened into sloping valleys of brown and green grass carpets. The elevation was high enough that the ocean twinkled at the western coastline. The beauty filled Lily with peace, but then she remembered how much Rose enjoyed the view, and her heart quickened.

She wished she could fly to the *Ard-Draoi*'s fortress, so that she could swiftly find Failinis and bring Rose home.

Atop Enbarr, Fintan studied the distant ocean, then looked around the pass. "What's this place called?"

Lily tucked hair behind her ear. "*Bealach Oisín.*"

Oisín's Pass.

Fintan hummed in appreciation. "The man must have hunted through this area many times to have a pass named after him." He patted his mount. "In fact, you know, he was carried away to the Otherworld on this very horse."

Lily blinked. She had known the stories but never made the connection. Chiding herself, she nodded with new purpose. Truly her mother's fanciful narratives were more than tales. More than just made-up stories to be passed onto children, who passed them onto their children.

What if some of them were true? Or all of them?

Fintan was right. The stories told of Enbarr, who had carried Oisín away to the Otherworld to live with Niamh. No one had seen Oisín since. His father, the famous warrior Fionn, had given up on his son's return and went down for the long sleep in an unknown cave. Only the *Borabu*, the hunting horn of the Fianna, could summon Fionn now.

It was still all hard for Lily to accept, especially when she thought about how the good folk, the faery, the gods, the goddesses, or anyone else with such powers could let Marigold drown in the ocean.

What fate had given Marigold the gift to speak with sea creatures, yet none helped her when she was taken beneath the wave?

Lily jerked her waterskin forward for a drink. "We stop for the last time today."

From here, she would set the route in a more westward direction versus their previous northward trek, then turn north again later. But because they would be too close to various settlements by the evening meal, she wouldn't risk a fire later or even stopping.

So, she set about making a hearty meal to fill up on now. Cúig sat back on his haunches, alternatively watching her gather brush for a fire and a herd of sheep crossing the path not more than twenty paces away. A few animals bleated as they hopped over slabs of rock sticking out of the ground.

Lily laughed at the bear's look of wonder. Not a country bear, obviously.

Meanwhile, Fintan found a boulder to use as a landing pad as he slid off Enbarr's back, and Ana washed her hands in a nearby stream. Once Lily had enough for her fire, she used the flint pouch to light the brush. She placed a small iron pot over the fire and filled it with water.

Soon enough they chowed on boiled tubers, oats, and barley. This would stick to the stomach a little longer, even if the little pot only provided enough to really satisfy two people.

Ana had sat close to Lily, blocking Cúig from being able to take his usual place by curling around her. When he sent Lily an image of slashing through Ana's dress with his claws, she shot him a look, eyebrows lowered. He huffed and found a patch of dried, springy grass to roll around in instead. Pleasured grunts followed, making Lily smile.

"I know a little about the *Ard-Draoi*, but I'm sure you have many questions." Ana nibbled a piece of dried bread. "I'm here for you. Whatever you need, my sweet."

Lily's eyes softened, some tension leaving her taut body. She realized then that she was terrified. Terrified of facing the powerful High Druid, terrified of going back to *Tír fo Thuinn*, terrified of losing Rose.

But Ana gave her courage. With the *bandraoi* at her side, she felt more in charge of herself, instead of slowly spiraling out of control. Ana had been there all her life. Even when the woman made her rounds to the many settlements, she had always made it a point to reconnect with Lily and her sisters every time she came home. Lily remembered summers of picking flowers, then braiding the colorful plants in each other's hair.

She loved Ana as much as her true mother.

Perhaps it was why Lily hadn't felt the loss of a father she never knew. When they had barely been over a year old, her father had died in service to their *taoiseach*, fighting in yet another battle for land. After that, her mother, grandmother, and Ana had always been there to see to all her and her sisters' needs.

Lily bit her lip, and then she asked a question she had asked herself a thousand times since Marigold had died. A question no one had been able to answer. But if anyone could come close, it would be Ana. "Why didn't the good folk save Marigold?"

Ana looked thoughtfully at her, the corners of her eyes drooping. "Perhaps her soul needed to be recycled for some greater purpose."

Recycled? Lily wasn't sure she believed in the concept. People reincarnating. Dead was dead. Besides, why would anyone want to live a life full of pain and regret yet again? Rose would chide her for thinking about any regrets. She always said regret was a wasteful emotion. Once more, Rose's favorite motto echoed in her mind.

"Cha d'dhùin doras nach d'fhosgail doras."

No door closed without another opening.

A loud snore interrupted her thoughts, and she smiled to see Cúig napping in the grass. Fintan also rested with his back against a boulder, his eye closed, chin to chest. Lily felt tired then, her sleepless night catching up to her. She rubbed fists over her eyes.

Ana poured her waterskin on the small fire. "Sometimes in one life you have to learn a lesson, one that you don't feel good about, but it will make you stronger for your next life."

Lily blew a piece of white-blonde hair out of her eyes while she kicked dirt over the ashes and embers. "If only you could remember those lessons between lives." She coughed, smoke irritating her raw throat.

"Some can remember, especially the reincarnated souls of the gods." Ana used a stick to stir the campfire remains, making sure everything was wet. Her pursed lips revealed to Lily that Ana knew something more about the subject but held back the information. Instead, Ana studied her, something crossing in her deep-brown eyes. "Are you ready to face the *Ard-Draoi* with your request?"

Lily's knuckles turned white as she cinched her laden satchel across her back. "I think so." She adjusted the harp and her spear, taking the spare weapon in hand. Then she considered Ana while the woman refilled her waterskin. "Have you ever met him?"

Ana didn't look at her. "Yes."

Lily raised her eyebrows, her nerves jumping. Even spending a lifetime with Ana, the *bandraoi* was full of surprises. "Is he really blind?"

One side of Ana's mouth quirked up. "Yes, he is blind as they say in the stories, and just as eccentric. He is as likely to have you thrown out just as quickly as he asks you to dance."

She swallowed. "Is he mean?"

Ana shook her head. "Not to me, but I don't fear him the way others do." She hesitated with her mouth open. "We've had a few disagreements, but there is nothing he can do to hurt me."

"How? He's the most powerful druid of our time."

Although a skilled and talented healer, Ana had admitted many times in the past that her magic did not compare to the average *draoi*, the other druids. It was part of the reason she wasn't stationed at any high-ranking *dúns* or fortresses.

She couldn't even do a locating spell to find Failinis. So, why wouldn't the High Druid be capable of hurting her?

Did she have a relationship with the High Druid? Is that why he wouldn't hurt her?

Her mother would be heartbroken if that was true.

Ana waved away her question, irritating her. Lily just wanted to know the truth. She bit her lip, summoning her courage to ask a different question.

"Are you lovers?"

Ana turned to fully face her, laughing.

"Not even close."

CHAPTER 19

COMING DOWN OUT OF THE mountains to gentler rolling plains made the pace quicken. The sky broke in a riot of colors as the sun slid behind the mountain range. A faint waft of salty ocean swirled on cooler winds.

If Lily closed her eyes, she could almost see the channel that ran along the northern shoreline where it skirted the *Ard-Draoi*'s island. Her stomach flipped a few times, and she wasn't sure whether it was because her time to see the High Druid was nearing or because she would have to face the very waters Marigold drowned in.

She led the group in a northwest direction, the land leveling with every pace gained toward the northern seashore of the peninsula. Lily avoided the clusters of settlements, warning silence among her companions. She knew the families who lived here. If anyone saw their party and recognized her, time would be wasted in trying to explain why she was traveling. She did not want the stares of compassion or sympathy at the loss of Marigold. It had only been a few short months, and Lily wasn't ready to deal with others talking about her sister's death.

After three more hours, with the moon rising over the waters of the channel, she approached one of the biggest settlements in the area. It belonged to her uncle, Ciara's older brother, and his extended family. Her uncle made a living on the water, casting nets every day to pull in as many fish as possible.

Salt lay heavy in the air here as Lily skirted the roundhouses and penned animals. They didn't have the walls of a *ráth*. Instead, their buildings spread out across the land. Past the most northern roundhouse, Lily trudged toward the white strands along the ocean. When her leather shoes hit the sandy beach, she stopped, her heart stalling in her chest.

Waves lapped the shore. A gentle breeze sighed. She stared across the water, where the ocean glinted in the moonlight. Waves caught each other in soft clashes.

The sound used to soothe her, lulling her to sleep.

But not now.

She recalled her memories from the last trip here. It had been a bright summer day when she and her sisters had been visiting their uncle and his family.

Marigold wanted to go swimming, as usual. She had twirled out the door of the roundhouse, throwing a wide smile at Lily. "I need to commune with my fishies."

While Lily could communicate with land animals and Rose with sky animals, Marigold could talk with water creatures, and the ocean provided a wealth of life not seen in their Salmon River back home.

Rose had decided to visit with one of their cousins, so it was just Lily and Marigold who kicked off their leather shoes and flirted with the laps of waves rolling along the beach. Then Marigold had stripped her dress off, leaving only a white linen tunic that hung just to her knees. Her golden curls bounced loose.

As usual, Marigold went a little farther until the sea's salty waters clung to her knees, then her upper thighs, and then her waist, the ocean swirling around her as she waded out. She laughed aloud.

"You don't see Rose trying to fly with the birds," Lily had yelled to her.

Marigold shrugged. Her arms spread wide. "Her loss!" Then she dove into the water.

By then, Lily had taken a seat out of the water's reach, leaning her head back to catch the warm sun on her neck. She smiled when Marigold reemerged, the water exploding in tiny eruptions all around her as fish danced and flipped in enjoyment. Marigold laughed.

That had been the last laugh Lily had ever heard from her sister.

A sudden shadow had loomed in the distance.

Lily scrambled to her feet. "Marigold!"

Her sister had looked at her and, seeing where she pointed, turned to see a wave building momentum toward her, rumbling as it rolled forward, cresting higher and higher. Lily had never seen anything like it before. It was so huge, it blotted out the sun at its highest peak. There was something unnatural about it, but she didn't have time to think about that.

She ran to the water as Marigold struggled to find footing in the shifting sand. The water sucked her backward. Then she slipped under the water with a scream.

"No!" Lily yelled for her sister, slugging through the salty sea. But a wave slapped her back, and she tumbled beneath the surface. Her arms and legs flailed around and sand scratched her face in the swirling waters.

Finally, her fingers felt the bottom, and she dragged herself to higher ground until she could plant her feet. She flung back toward the water, screaming for Marigold.

The sea's now placid surface barely crested in tiny waves. It was as if that huge wave couldn't have existed in such calm waters.

She swam up and down the coastline, calling out Marigold's name repeatedly, tears flowing freely. She scrambled to the bank, falling a few times, tangled in her soggy trousers, but she got right back up, wading out into the water. She plunged into the depths, searching the ocean floor for some sign—Marigold's white tunic or her honey-colored hair.

Soon, Lily's tears were indistinguishable from the rivulets of water streaming over her face as she dove back into the water over and over again, hoarsely calling out for her sister.

When limbs grew heavy, she crawled onto the beach and sobbed. Tears lumped in her throat, and she gasped for air. The taste and smell of salt clogged all her senses.

An hour later, Rose found her dragging through the water again, sobbing, calling for Marigold with sounds that were no longer recognizable. Lily looked to her sister, feeling lost.

For several moments, Rose had stood there, horror creeping across her features as she realized what had happened. Lily turned away, back to the ocean, calling out for Marigold, her voice broken. Rose joined her.

She wasn't sure how long they searched for their lost sister, but eventually, Rose pulled her away with an arm around her shoulders.

Lily yearned to turn back but shrunk into Rose's body. She felt numb when she spoke. "I should have gone out with her."

She didn't know if Rose had blamed her in that moment. She'd felt so much despair, but she wouldn't have been upset if Rose had. She should have done more.

The memory faded, but Lily knew it would sneak up on her again. She scrubbed tears trickling down her cheeks and stared at the calm night waters in front of her.

Could she cross now?

She wanted to. She wanted to finish this part of her mission to start the next, finding Lugh's dog. Then she could rescue Rose.

She took a step toward small waves lapping the pale strand. She waited for her old fear to surface, but although her heart skipped a beat, she kept her hands from shaking, and her stomach quivered only a little.

Fintan sidled close to her. "Enbarr can cross water as if walking on land."

Lily raised eyebrows at him. Then she recalled the myths. Interesting and useful. She eyed the horse and the animal's capacity to ferry them all. "It would take a while for her to take us all across." She would have to make a couple of trips. She glanced at her furry companion. Cúig sat on his back haunches, his forepaws crossed in front of him. Could he swim? "How would the bear cross?"

Fintan flicked his nose with one gnarled thumb. "I can take care of the rest of us. You ride Enbarr."

Her stomach flipped.

She had grown so attached to Cúig that she couldn't think of leaving him behind, but maybe he shouldn't follow her. What could possibly change if he didn't go with her? But even as she tried to communicate this to him, he moaned a great deal and shook his shaggy head. She bit her lip, then looked back across the water. "Fine, you silly bear. Come if that pleases you."

The old man stepped up to the water's edge, bending to touch the waves. His voice was so low that Lily had to strain to hear the words.

"Master of the Sea, Father of Swans, Holder of Traditions, hear me now. Father, answer me with your sea vessel."

Dark clouds moved across the moon's surface, speeding faster than Lily had ever seen. They built up in shape and size, blotting out the celestial body. Temperatures dropped rapidly. She pulled the ends of her cloak closer together. Then a streak of lightning snaked through the clouds, lighting up the sky. Another sparked closer, then another. They continued until they were no more than twenty paces away. The last one left the clouds to strike the top of the ocean's water. The light was so blinding that Lily had to throw an arm across her eyes.

When she tried to look to the water again, her vision danced with small dots of light. Eventually, the brightness receded, and forms began to take shape again. The old man stood in the water, tugging a small boat toward him. He hauled the boat to the edge of the water, keeping a hand on it as it floated inches above the sand.

Ana inspected the currach. It was a small fishing boat made of sticks and animal hide. "*Sguaba Tuinne*, Wave-Sweeper." Her tone suggested that she was neither surprised nor impressed. Her pale hands gripped the edges of her gray cloak, but her face was passive while she perused the old man. "Who is your father?"

"Lir," was his simple reply.

The answer shocked Lily. *The Tuatha Dé Danann's Sea God was the old man's father?* Of course, Fintan himself was legend, but no one had known his parentage, only that he had married Noah's granddaughter. Then it made sense. That was why he could change form in his stories, with his favorite being the fish, which was how he survived the world's great flood.

Ana stepped inside the boat, the old man shoving the currach farther into the water as it sank before motioning for the bear and climbing inside himself. It was a perfect fit for the three of them, growing in size to what the group needed.

Meanwhile, Lily climbed atop Enbarr after sending her a message for her to kneel again. When the horse had gained her feet, she stepped onto the water without hesitation and didn't sink. Lily released her breath. Even though magic had infused almost all her waking moments for the last two days, much of it was still hard to comprehend at times.

Enbarr galloped toward the island of Dairbhre. *Sguaba Tuinne* gathered speed, navigating itself, until it crashed through the waves alongside the horse. Ahead in the darkness, Lily could barely discern the outline of the island. The moon had not yet peeked back out from the cloud cover, so she leaned against Enbarr's neck, sending her a message. It was an image of the island and the section for the safest landing. Long parts of the coastline were either giant slabs of limestone or jagged rock.

No more than a few minutes passed when the horse finally slowed. The sound of water quieted to small laps. Then Enbarr stopped, not even breathing hard. Moments later, the boat pulled onto the beach at the water's edge.

Lily dismounted, smelling the woodsy aroma of oak trees beneath the scent of the salty ocean. Cúig bounded from the watercraft. When Fintan and Ana stepped out, the boat shrunk in size and shifted itself back into the water, disappearing in a mist that evaporated seconds after covering the boat.

Lily flexed her fingers, considering whether to pull a spear out, then dismissed the idea. Wouldn't do to put the *Ard-Draoi* on alert. She glanced at Ana, a dark figure on the beach. "Do you know the way to Mug Ruith's fortress?"

Twinkling light appeared around Ana, illuminating several paces around her. The bandraoi smiled when Lily gaped because she had never seen the magic Ana used now.

"A simple spell for all druids." The older woman tilted her head back, looking further into the island. "This way."

Ana's command spurred Lily to follow, Cúig and Fintan falling close behind. It was hard enough to see with the moon covered and mist bubbled all along the ground, so they stayed close to the only light source, the twinkling lights hovering just around Ana.

Leaving the beach behind, they entered the grove of oak trees at a slight incline. Lily recognized a quick series of high-pitched barks and opened her mind to interact with the nocturnal foxes. The barks subsided, replaced with the low hum of insects. Wind shifted tree branches and dried leaves with a quick cadence.

Lily pulled her cloak ends closer together. It was colder on the island, and the higher they climbed, the more wind gushed by them. "Do you think Mug Ruith knows we're here?"

"He knows." Ana gestured with one hand, her twinkling lights shifting outward.

Lily peered through the forest.

Lights farther inland and uphill wound their way toward Lily and her group. The unknown illumination neared until a pair of men came into view on their path. They were hooded in brown robes, so Lily couldn't see their faces, but one cried out at seeing them.

"*Cailleach!*"

The next few minutes slowed down to moments that seemed incomprehensible to Lily.

Light twinkled around the two men like Ana, but they waved their hands in large circles, showing arms with various circular tattoos.

An invisible band wrapped around Lily's entire body so that she couldn't move. Behind her, Cúig roared. In front of her, Ana rotated her wrists.

The men's hoods flipped back, revealing the faces of young men with long, dark hair held back by thin bronze bands. Their eyes bulged, and suddenly, their arms fell limp at their sides.

Ana stepped up to them.

"You would call me a hag but call yourselves druids. Such naivete will cause you trouble." She made a tsk sound. "You should have thought twice about taking an offensive against someone who could prove more powerful than you."

Lily's mouth fell open, then something heavy landed in her stomach as Ana's words penetrated her shock. The *bandraoi* casually intimated that her magic could overcome the druids', but how could that be true? These were druids working for the *Ard-Draoi*, and Ana had admitted on numerous occasions that her magic had limitations.

Both men shared a glance, but their faces remained impassive. One of the young men had a straggly mustache on his upper lip. He met Ana's stare. "What business do you have on *Oileán Dairbhre*?"

Ana turned away from them, tracking back to Lily. Her hands hovered over Lily's body, but the *bandraoi* refused to meet her eyes. Lily clenched her jaw, but then jerked as the invisible band holding her immobile vanished. Ana swished away to work on Fintan's and Cúig's hidden bonds.

The entire time, Lily studied Ana. Watching her.

The woman was a mystery. Not something Lily would have ever thought about her second mother before today.

When Ana didn't respond to the druid's question, Lily answered. "We need an immediate audience with Mug Ruith."

Now Ana returned to stand before the two druids, her hands hovering a last time to release their invisible restrictions. Still, she said nothing, only motioning for the men to lead the way.

Lily walked cautiously behind her mentor, her mother's lover. A sickening feeling tumbled in her middle. *Ana was not who she said she was.*

Ana was much more powerful than Lily had ever imagined. The *bandraoi* openly admitted to the druids that she was more capable than them. Then there was that comment about the High Druid not being able to hurt her.

Was it possible that Ana could have easily helped Lily find Failinis, helped Lily save Rose?

Bile came up her throat.

Who was Ana?

Her friend, her mentor, her second mother.

A liar.

CHAPTER 20

LESS THAN A QUARTER HOUR had passed when the trees thinned. In a large grassy plain, an earthen bank had been built up around a dark, imposing structure. As they neared, a huge fortress of stone rose out of the very ground. Wooden gates groaned open. The sound echoed across the plain.

They passed beneath a stone archway to enter a *lis* entirely covered in stone blocks inlaid along the ground. Although many smaller buildings resided in shadow, the imposing stone fortress towered toward the night sky.

Lily had never seen anything like it. Not even *Clann Séaghdha*'s chief's main fortress was so dominating. The building had to be at least a couple dozen paces high and was created entirely of cut stone blocks, each block at least three paces in length and width. Giants had to be responsible for building it. How else could such huge stones be moved and stacked on top of each other?

A dozen torches lit their path to the massive doorway with two posted sentries who nodded and pulled the doors open.

Lily's heart leapt. In moments, she'd face the High Druid and ask for his help.

She glanced at Ana. At first the woman provided security in her quest, but now Lily didn't know what to trust. She took a deep breath.

What else was the *bandraoi* hiding?

Did Ciara know?

Her heart hurt at the thought of Ana's deception toward her mother.

Lily glanced one last time at the moon sitting low in the night sky. Would this be her last moonrise? She couldn't possibly know what the

Ard-Draoi would want from her in return for the information she needed, but she thought she was prepared.

Her steps lagged inside, then she berated herself for being a coward. Throwing back her shoulders, she took longer steps to catch up to her guides, who had breezed past the doorway and disappeared into the hallway ahead as if the building were a whale swallowing its evening meal.

Ana sauntered ahead, but Cúig walked on all fours next to her. Behind her, Fintan tapped along with his staff, looking more haggard than she'd ever seen him since knowing him.

The long hallway passed a multitude of rooms with closed wooden doors. Then a central spacious room opened from the hallway. It was filled with weapons hanging on the walls, carved seats, and beautifully decorated rugs. A low fire burned in a stone hearth that seemed to ventilate smoke through a narrow channel leading up the side of the wall.

Did the channel open outside?

It would have to, or smoke would fill the room, which happened with the wrong wind even in roundhouses that had a central opening in the roof.

Lily shortened her stride after she caught up to the druids. She passed through yet another hallway, this one shorter and with stone steps on both sides that spiraled up out of sight.

She instinctively ducked at the thought of rooms above her head.

How did the structure support all the weight of these huge stones and not come crashing down on everyone? What kept the building stable?

The sound of a woman's laughter floated to where Lily had paused by the stone stairs. She took a few tentative steps away, toward the scent of roast pig and honeyed tubers. Bright light spilled out from the room ahead and as Lily stepped from the hallway, cinnamon and cloves also wafted toward her.

It was a banquet hall.

A long table covered in a snow-white cloth piled high with more food than all the people in her *ráth* could eat in a day. Several men sat at the table, many wearing brown or black robes with bronze bands holding back their long hair. Two people caught her eye.

One she recognized instantly. The beautiful Greek woman, Hera, sat facing the doorway near the head of the table. Candlelight gleamed in her smiling eyes. Delicate gold earrings swung against her bare neck as she laughed. Her long, dark hair was swept up in an artful arrangement of curls, which brushed her cheeks and cascaded down the center of her back under a transparent veil. A single peacock feather was pinned to the side of her head.

Several of her Greek soldiers lined the wall behind her, likely their attention focused on the guests and Hera's safety.

At Hera's right, at the head of the table, sat a man with the strangest appearance. A hornless bull hide graced his shoulders, resting on top a tunic finer than any Lily had ever seen, even by the wealthiest men of her clan. A bird mask hid most of his face, leaving only a bearded chin open. When he lifted a bit of food to his hidden mouth, it was beneath the bird's very real, very long, curved beak.

The bird mask turned toward her, showing the bird eyelids sewn shut. The man's blind stare took the group's measure. Hera stilled, her previous laughter dying. The others also quieted at their entrance, hands of dinner guests lowering and hands of guards hovering nearer weapons.

The druid guides stopped several paces from the table. The mustached one spoke. "*Ollamh Draoi*, these visitors have insisted on seeing you right away."

The *Ard-Draoi* lifted a white linen cloth to the mouth hidden beneath the curved beak before resting his hands on the grand table. When he spoke, a faint smile touched his voice. "A girl of mysterious origins, a woman hiding her real face, a man thought dead, and a man in bear's clothing."

Lily scrunched her face, biting her lip. His description puzzled her. Being the girl of mysterious origins didn't fit her. She knew exactly where she came from. Ana must be the woman hiding her real face. Before today, Lily would not have agreed with him. Of course, Fintan was the man thought dead, and that left the bear. She wasn't sure what the High Druid's remark meant about him.

She cleared her throat and stepped in front of Ana, who had led the way into the banquet hall. "*Ard-Draoi*, I offer myself in whatever service you require in return for your help to see my sister's safe return from the Otherworld."

At first, silence met her words, then a woof resounded off the stone ceiling as Hera's beautiful, parti-colored greyhound jumped to his feet at the woman's side. He wagged his tail at seeing Lily, and the corners of Lily's mouth quirked up at him.

The *Ard-Draoi* swept a hand over the table. "Welcome to *Cloch na Coille*, the Woodstone fortress. Please, join us in this sumptuous meal."

Lily blinked. That was not the response she'd expected, but Cúig emitted a low huff, his thoughts clear to her. He'd love to eat. Then, Jason padded around the table toward her, and she pet his smooth head, while keeping an eye on the High Druid and Hera.

Did Hera recognize her?

While the Greek woman's dark eyes perused them, her face revealed little of her thoughts. She laid a hand on the High Druid's arm. "I don't think that is a good idea."

Cúig groaned, plopping back on his haunches.

It was hard to tell what the powerful druid felt with the bird mask covering his face, but he shook off the woman's hand. His blind bird gaze lingered on Lily and her group as he rubbed a finger and thumb over his bearded chin. "Surely you can make time to eat."

Lily opened her mouth at the same time Jason nudged his nose into her hand. She frowned at him as he sent her the golden image of a human's silhouette. The very same image he'd given her when they'd first met.

Then Ana jumped in while Lily had been distracted, her eyes on Hera, but her question for the High Druid. "Why do you harbor Éire's enemy in your home?"

A collective gasp echoed at the accusation. Hera's brow furrowed and Ana's mouth tightened. From the corner of her eye, Lily watched Fintan move back toward the hallway.

She turned her own wide-eye stare on the women. *Did they know each other?*

The *Ard-Draoi* threw back his head and chortled. "What fun we have. The goddess reveals herself."

No one joined in the laugh.

CHAPTER 21

THE GODDESS? *Who did the High Druid refer to?*

Lily bit her lip while watching the two women before her.

Ana fisted her hands on her hips. "This woman will encourage the destruction of our ways."

Jason suddenly bumped Lily again, and his projected images swept over her in a tidal wave too strong to resist. She swayed on her feet from the onslaught. The golden silhouette in his vision resolved into a man, love surrounding him and emanating from him. Lily couldn't separate the love that flew from dog to man and from man to dog. It was evident that the pair cared deeply about each other.

When Lily's eyesight cleared, she found herself kneeling next to Jason, his pink tongue lapping her face. She pitched her voice low. "What are you trying to tell me?"

"You are nothing but carrion filth, living for the blood of others..." Hera stood now, her thin body trembling and her olive complexion flushed a deep red color. Her chin tilted up while she looked down on Ana.

Lily stood. Jason sat at her feet, his intelligent brown eyes trained on her face. Not knowing what he wanted, she looked to the *bandraoi*, who vibrated with tension next to her.

Ana stalked deliberately toward the table, her eyes locked on Hera. "You are one to speak, wreaking havoc on mortals for a mere laugh..."

Cúig took advantage of Ana's seeming attack and stomped up to the table with a roar. Hera waved a hand to shoo him back, and the bear spun across the room, slamming into the wall. Dust rained downed from the stone ceiling. Cúig shook his head in confusion.

Hera smiled. "Dumb animal."

Surprised, a little fearful, and getting very angry, Lily unlatched the harp on her back. She hadn't known that Hera was capable of magic, but she didn't like her friends getting hurt.

The *Ard-Draoi* shot to his feet. He held up a hand. "No magic."

Ana ignored him as she raised a finger to point at Hera. "I told you what could happen if you didn't leave."

A spark lanced from her fingertip, but Hera waved a hand, and it slammed into the stone wall behind her, leaving a jagged black mark across its surface, inches from one of her Greek soldier's faces.

Lily swallowed. For the first time, she was glad Ana was a powerful druid. But could she stand up to Hera's abilities? What about the High Druid?

Hera jerked her chin up with a triumphant smile, her curls bouncing on her shoulders. A purple glow outlined the woman. "I don't take orders from you."

"This is my land."

Black mists rolled along the ground.

The *Ard-Draoi* slammed his fists onto the table. "Ladies, I will not tolerate..."

Now Hera ignored him. "And I will stay if I so choose."

Ana balled her fists. "Do you really want to test me? You have no contest against me in my own land. I will squeeze out the golden blood running through your veins until every drop sows the lands of Éire. When I'm done with you, not even ambrosia will heal your—"

Hera slapped her palms on the table, her nostrils flaring. For the first time, Lily found the woman had lost her natural beauty. "I will bring war to these lands once my husband finds out about your threats."

Ana threw her head back with a malicious laugh. "You mean the husband who doesn't know you're chasing a lover through my country?"

Hera sniffed, settling back on her heels and crossing her arms. The purple glow continued to shine around her. "He will not stand for an attack against me."

Now Ana planted her hands on the table and leaned toward the Greek woman. She stressed every word. "I don't care."

Lightning sparks suddenly snapped between the two women, but both easily waved away the strikes, and the charges bounced away from them, flying in all directions. The other druids grunted as they flung out of their seats and ducked while the Greek soldiers slammed to the floor. Electrical charges crashed into the wall. Rebound fragments struck the ceiling and the floor. Long black gashes appeared all over the room.

Lily crouched near Jason, harp in her hands, watching the light show. The dog whimpered as he leaned into her. Behind her, Cúig covered Fintan with his body.

Just as Lily thought to play the harp, Mug Ruith placed his hands on each woman's shoulder, pushing them apart. "Enough!"

The sparks stopped.

So, the High Druid did have some control. Why hadn't he intervened before? Perhaps he enjoyed the confrontation.

The druid men and Greek soldiers groaned as they resumed their seats or stood back against the walls.

Both women looked surprised, perhaps forgetting that they had an audience. The Ard-Draoi focused on Ana. "Hera is my guest and so has my protection extended to her. Don't break the bonds and words of our hospitality laws."

Ana backed up a step but tsked loudly at Hera. "Coward. Hiding behind the magic of a druid."

Hera bared her teeth. "I have no need to hide."

The *Ard-Draoi* sighed. "No one is hiding."

"I would crush you without the druid's protection." Ana sneered.

"Highly unlikely."

"Then meet me outside these walls."

Abruptly, Hera seemed interested in the gold polish on her nails. Her face returned to its normal olive tone and the purple glow faded. "I am not here to fight. I have more important things to do."

Her eyes unexpectedly locked with Lily's, but if the Greek woman remembered her, she showed no sign of it. Instead, her gaze flickered to her dog. "Jason, come."

The dog didn't move or wag his tail.

Ana laughed. "Even the dog yearns to get away from you, just like your lost lover."

A new wave of deep red swept over Hera's skin, and she flicked one wrist in the air in a precise and quick movement with a minute show of violet light.

An invisible smack cracked in the air.

Ana's hand shot up to her face, rubbing her cheek. A crimson handprint marred her pale skin. Ever so slowly, a weird smile curled the ends of her lips. "An attack on me negates the High Druid's protection."

Swiftly, both women raised their hands at the same time. Purple light filtered through a black mist. The *Ard-Draoi* shrugged back his animal hide and held up his hands, a verdant light encircling him.

The druids ducked again. Hera's soldiers rushed forward with swords unsheathing. Cúig roared.

A new round of sparks electrified the air. Dishes crashed to the floor.

This time, Lily dropped to the stone ground, the harp pulled tight against her body. She closed her eyes. The smell of sulfur tickled her nose. Then she plucked the harp's strings, fingertips playing a song. She hummed to the harp's tune.

Her fingers kept moving until she no longer heard any bodies dropping to the ground, until Jason's growling had subsided, until Ana's screech silenced.

When she opened her eyes, the room was asleep.

Only Jason and Cúig remained alert, being the sole animals in the room. Lily quirked half a smile. That meant the harp only worked on people, except for her, of course, as the one to play the music. She hadn't known those details from the stories.

She stowed the harp in the harness on her back then kneeled next to Jason, massaging his ear while she thought through her options. "I guess I wait for the *Ard-Draoi* to awaken." She eyed the sleeping druid and had the urge to run. What if he was mad at her? But maybe he'd look favorably on her for stopping the lightning war. "So that leaves the question of what can we do about Ana and Hera?"

Jason tilted his head at her with a whine. Cúig sniffed the air, his tongue flicking out. He approached the table and snatched a piece of roast pig.

She stood, wiping her hands on her trousers. Dust littered the air. Perhaps if she got the High Druid alone, she'd be able to request his help the right way. She circled the table to where he slumped over and pulled on one of his arms.

The man slid to the floor with a loud thump.

She winced.

Hopefully he wouldn't have too big a knot from his head hitting the stone floor.

She flipped him over, her intention to drag him into another room away from the two fighting women. But as she grabbed the thin-shouldered man under the arms, Jason nipped her hand.

She yelped. Cúig glanced curiously at her. Then she massaged her hand with a frown at the dog. "What's wrong?"

He sat back and lifted a paw, so she sighed. She swept her hand over his head, and he leaned into her palm as she scratched behind his ear. She relayed her mission to the hound as best as she could through images, impressing her need to free Rose from the leprechaun.

Immediately, he flooded her with the image of the golden man again. Lily squeezed her eyes shut. By giving her the same image multiple times, the hound was trying to communicate a message that he felt she should understand.

But who was the man? She couldn't see his face.

She leaned her head against the dog's forehead, hoping for more.

Then it came to her.

A story of Balor, king of the Fomorians, oppressors to the Tuatha Dé Danann. He bemoaned the return of his prophesied grandson who would kill him in battle. "Today the sun rose in the west, so bright was this warrior's approach upon me, blinding me like sudden sunlight in shadow."

This bringer of sunlight, this golden Lugh.

CHAPTER 22

PILES OF SILVER AND GOLD coins, silver and gold artifacts, gems shimmering with every rainbow hue, and countless objects of immense value filled the back chamber of the cave. Tapering stalactites in the high ceiling dripped bits of moisture, while stalagmites intermittently rose out of the heaps of treasure like teeth chomping on an expensive meal.

Peering over the stockpile of precious metals and gems, Lugh decided he needed more. Paiste the dragon eyed him, his long, sinuous black body woven in-between the treasure mounds. The creature curled the ends of his mouth over ferocious-looking teeth.

Lugh clapped his hands and danced a quick jig. "Ready for a ride, my friend?"

Paiste's yellow eyes rolled around the cavern. Smoke leaked from his scaly lips. "I would love to add to my fortunes."

Lugh smiled. "To Éire we go!"

Then he returned to the main entrance of the cave, leaving the dragon to find his way out through the mountain's tunnel system.

A full morning sun slanted light rays through the glass walls.

He could smell the sun, breathing it full in. It smelled like raspberries and ale.

Although the sun here in *Tír fo Thuinn* was never as strong as it was in the other lands of the Otherworld, he appreciated the continual celestial body, even though it entered a twilight phase.

A clink of a chain drew his attention, and he scowled.

Mousie had stood as he entered the room. Her pet eagle hopped along the ground. Lugh narrowed his eyes on the bird. *Who was he?*

He pat his red coat, thinking to find answers.

He couldn't remember where he put them.

"Will you remove my chains?" Mousie interrupted him. "I need to relieve myself."

Again, he narrowed his eyes on the red-haired sorceress. What would he do with her? He itched to just be done with the insipid nuisance. Perhaps killing her now would relieve him.

A solitary person by nature, he wasn't used to having someone always around. Unless it was his hound.

His beloved hound! Failinis.

No, he had to wait. No killing today.

Somehow, now he wasn't suddenly as irritated by her presence. Perhaps because she was a promise of his missing hound.

But if she insisted on saying his name, she would wish she was dead.

He swept his hand toward her, and a wind pushed her back against the wall.

"Oh," she said, catching her balance.

He ignored her frown and chuckled low. Did she pee in her trousers? He quickly looked her over but thinking about what lay beneath her clothing sent heat up his neck. He cleared his throat to clear the images from his mind. "Ready for a new adventure?"

"What will I be this time?"

The question sent him into a round of belly laughs.

What fun he had changing her!

A mouse, a he-she leprechaun, a rabbit—he had fun watching her little pink nose twitch as the eagle had chased her—and a ladybug, which amused him for over an hour as she kept running into the glass walls.

He scratched the beard line on his cheek, his head tilted as he thought about what to make her.

"Leave me as myself," she said.

"Bloody Dagda's balls, you are a monster in that form." He withdrew his Druid rod and stalked toward her, his grin widening as he closed the distance. He had the perfect idea.

She clenched her hands together and the eagle gave a shrill whistle. It pleased him to see the fear in her eyes as she followed him, wondering what he would do to her next. Then Lugh touched the rod to her white-knuckled hands. A bright light enveloped her and seconds later, she turned into a greyhound dog, one that looked very much like his beloved Failinis, but she was a russet color all over and only a quarter of the size.

The dog looked down at herself and whined.

Lugh chuckled. "Come, dog."

He cuffed her on the ear before leading the way outside, where Paiste waited. Mousie's eyes grew wide at the sight of the black creature. She whimpered once, then squatted on the grass to relieve herself. When she was done, Lugh snapped his fingers, calling for her to approach the dragon with him.

She whimpered again, squatting one more time.

Lugh cuffed her behind her ear again, the ear point flopping over. She yelped and stumbled, then slinked on her belly close toward Paiste.

"That's a good dog." He pat her on the head.

He climbed atop the sinuous back, using one of the dragon's legs as an aid. He snapped to Mousie, and she jumped up in front of him. He wrapped his arms around her to hold her close, and the dragon began a steady run through the forest.

The wind lashed his beard all around, and he grumbled, but soon enough they came to a still pond, that stretched only ten paces across. The dragon did not stop his forward motion but dove right into the water and down under the surface.

When they emerged, the dragon climbed onto the bank of a fast-moving river. A forest surrounded them on all sides, with a sun peeking in and out of clouds above. Moisture lingered in the air. Lugh took a deep breath, smelling wet soil. A rainstorm had just passed.

Perfect! Paiste knew how to pick them.

There were so many ways to find treasure. The usual way was to steal it from those who were frivolous with their wealth. Sometimes he found treasure when he mended shoes. Charitable people would often leave their precious coins or jewels sitting out for him to find. He took it for payment.

But his favorite way of hunting treasure was the pot at the end of a rainbow.

The dragon hunkered down by the river as Lugh raised a hand to the sky. The clouds shifted along, allowing the sun its full reign, and as it glared through the sky, a rainbow appeared in the distance.

"Run fast, Paiste," he said.

The beast lunged forward, trees and grass a blur beneath his body until the dragon caught the beginning of the rainbow, the red, orange, yellow, green, blue, and violet stripes twinkling a welcome at him. The dragon's sides huffed as he came to a stop, black scales glinting in the sunlight.

Lugh dismounted, tugging Mousie with him. The side of his mouth twitched as she tumbled and tried to gain a stable ground under her four legs. Unfortunately, he needed to transform her from this lovely hound. He liked this version of her. A reminder of his missing hound.

With the Druid rod, he refashioned her. Her form shrunk in length but grew in height to match his. She was back in her he-she leprechaun form, complete with wide hips and red beard. "You can only walk a rainbow as a leprechaun."

Then he stepped onto the tail of the multi-hued rainbow where it touched the ground. Paiste stayed on behind, curling around the colors to guard the rainbow's beginning, keep it in place long enough for them to return. Mousie took small steps to follow, and Lugh thought he might have to prod her along. But when he raised his hand, she squeaked and leapt for the tail.

As he walked, his feet stuck to the surface, so that at the beginning, his body was parallel with the ground, but he didn't fall. This assurance didn't help Mousie.

Or his nerves!

She continually squeaked and even whimpered like the dog she'd been.

Gods, why hadn't he chosen today to kill her?

"Blubbering idiot," he said to her. He grabbed her hand. "You'll not fall."

Her wide blue eyes looked down as the land fell further away. He followed her gaze. The world was beautiful this far up. So green, even in winter, with blue sinuous lines and pools for the rivers and lakes. White clouds passed between him and the earth, and he marveled at their puffiness.

Mousie ripped her hand from his and fell to her knees. She leaned over the side of the rainbow and spewed the contents of her stomach. Mostly water with a few chunks of soggy bread.

Lugh couldn't contain his laughter for so many reasons, one of course for the fool girl getting sick. He slapped his knees and stomped his feet. He wished he could be there when her vomit landed on some unsuspecting person. Imagine if it fell all over the laundry hanging up to dry after a good washing! Perhaps it would splash over a pig who would squeal and run maddeningly through the fields.

His laughter eventually faded, and he continued the climb. Mere moments later, he passed the halfway mark so that the rainbow angled downward. Soon he faced the ground for the last leg of the journey. When he glanced over his shoulder and saw Mousie's green face, he pushed her ahead of him.

No way she'd puke all over the back of him.

A few moments later, she purged her insides again.

It was watery.

They were still too far up for Lugh to see where it landed, but he tried to follow the fall of the vomit for as long as he could, laughing in sprints.

When he finally reached the ground, jumping the last couple of paces from the rainbow's end to go up and over the pot of treasures, he swung his head around to find the puke, but the wind must have carried it away.

Twisting his lips with a sigh, he rubbed his hands together. Now it was time to collect the precious metals and jewels.

He whipped out his brown sack.

"Mousie, grab the treasure and put it all in here, including the cauldron."

She looked doubtfully at him, her pale face finally gaining color now that they were on solid ground. The pot was bigger than his small sack. "Why didn't the dragon just bring us here instead of dropping us off at the other end of the rainbow?"

"You really know nothing!"

He gestured the open sack at her, and she grabbed the pot's black rim, hauling it toward him.

Blowing out a huff of exasperation, he deigned to answer her question. "Treasure only stays put at the end of the rainbow by walking to it from the beginning of the rainbow."

"Oh."

Now she tipped the cauldron inside. As she did, the pot shrunk in size, so that when it vanished, the brown sack only had a slight bulge the size of two fists.

Lugh threw the sack on his shoulder, began a whistle, and took one step onto the rainbow. A familiar squeak made him turn around, a frown forming as he put together a scathing comment for Mousie, but then he stopped.

A large man, standing at least six feet tall, gripped Mousie around the neck with one big, hairy hand. He picked her up to hold her to his face level, her small hands flailing at his one. "You're the ugliest leprechaun I ever did see."

Lugh's face flamed. "Hideous beast wouldn't know beautiful if it slapped your nana in the tits."

The man sputtered, then narrowed his eyes. "Take me to your treasure or I shall squeeze the life out of this one."

Mousie's face turned a weird shade of purple. Panic filled Lugh's chest. She was his! Only he could kill her. "You'll kill her before I get you to my treasure. Here, have this." He threw his sack with the rainbow's pot of gold and gems.

The man gave a short laugh. "I know you have more than that, but..." He set Mousie on her feet again, keeping a fist in her long, curly red hair. "Show me the rest."

"Fine." Lugh set off into the forest, his mind thinking and jumping to ideas while on his imaginary path to his hoard of riches. Behind him, the man yanked Mousie along. Tears leaked from her large, blue eyes as she held onto her hair where the man clutched.

That made Lugh furious. His lips flattened and heat flushed his body.

What could he do to be rid of the man and keep Mousie safe?

Then the idea came to him.

He picked out one tree in the distance. "Almost there." When he came to the base of the tree, he stopped. "Here, you festering gumboil, you will find my entire treasure buried in front of this tree. All you need to do is dig it up."

The man scratched his head with a free hand, the other still in Mousie's hair. "Why can't you dig it up?"

Lugh opened his red coat. "Do I look like I carry a shovel, blind lubberwort?"

The man looked at the ground for several blank moments. When he had an answer to the dilemma, his whole face lit up. "I will mark the tree and come back later for it."

Lugh shrugged and moved a hand through the air. "By all means, whatever you must do. Just be done with it, bursting blister."

The man's face turned a deep shade of purple, but he released Mousie and hurriedly stripped off his gray woolen trousers. Mousie turned away, her cheeks pink. Then the man tore the trousers into one long strip, using this to tie completely around the tree, knotting them tightly and testing the bonds several times.

"I'll be back." He retreated quickly, running through the forest the way they'd come, his bare backside flashing them as his tunic flapped up and down.

The minute he was far enough away that he wouldn't overhear them, Lugh went to Mousie and swept back her hair and beard. Her breath sounded labored. Red and purple splotches in the shape of the man's fingers marred the pale skin of her neck. Lips tight, Lugh touched the end of his beard to the marks, and they faded. The girl's breathing slowed and the raspiness eased.

"Better?"

She returned his earnest gaze, something like wonder in her eyes, but he dismissed it. She nodded, and he released her, looking around at the surrounding trees.

"Is there really treasure buried here?"

"No, witless mouse." He ran both his hands over his beard several times, and then raised them high overhead. In a flash of light, every tree in range of the original one had an identical pair of gray trousers, all facing the same way with the same exact knot.

Mousie's mouth dropped open.

"Clever leprechaun," she whispered.

He gave her a wink, and she blushed. He realized then that was the first time he ever treated her as a real person rather than his possession. He liked the warm feeling in his chest. Goose pimples raised along his arms.

Then he stilled as someone crashed through the forest.

It was the same offensive man, running until he caught up to them. The large oaf stopped to catch his breath, his eyes closed until he could breathe normally again. Then he glanced at Lugh as he straightened to his full height. "I should have asked, but does the other leprechaun also have treasure?" His eyes wandered around the forest as he spoke, the words trailing off. Bright-red streaks colored his face and neck. "What is going on?"

Lugh grabbed Mousie's sleeve and backed away from the man.

"You think to trick me?" He bared his teeth. "I remember which tree I marked, because you're still standing next to it." He stepped up to the tree and yanked at the gray trousers. "I'll just take my mark off, and it'll be the only one without it. Then I'll keep you both with me until I get a shovel."

The trousers finally released its knot, but as the legs slid around the tree, they moved as if having a life of their own. They flung around the man, wrapping him over and over with so many layers that the original trousers couldn't have had so much cloth to them. The man fell over with a large crash. Birds flew into the air.

When the gray trousers finished its job, the man was wrapped entirely except for his head. His face colored a brilliant shade of red.

Lugh grasped Mousie's hand, and they calmly walked away, the man cursing behind their backs.

Lugh laughed and even Mousie chuckled.

CHAPTER 23

LILY SAT BACK ON HER HEELS in the High Druid's banquet hall, holding the hound's head in her hands, searching his brown eyes. Hope ballooned in her chest. Then she tried the name that came to her lips.

"Failinis?"

The dog gave a low bark and licked her hand.

"Oh, now you're sorry for biting me?"

But she was so happy that she threw her arms around him with a laugh. She was going to save Rose, and she didn't even need the *Ard-Draoi*.

The golden man image radiated in her mind. She reflected the image of Lugh the leprechaun and Failinis whined.

No wonder she hadn't recognized Lugh before in the hound's mind. Failinis only saw his master as the glorious god. She dropped her arms. *How had he come to be in Hera's possession?* "You never looked like a Jason anyway."

He licked her face, which she scrubbed away with a shoulder as she stood. "C'mon. Let's get you back to Lugh."

With Failinis and Cúig by her side, they traversed back through the stone fortress, not a single sound echoing except for their footfalls. Everyone was asleep.

She questioned how far the harp's magic extended, because even the people in the *lis* were fast asleep. Grabbing a lit torch from outside, Lily exited the *ráth* and led the way back through the oaken forest and down to the sandy beach.

There she found Enbarr.

She could ride the horse back to *Tír fo Thuinn*, but how would the hound and Cúig get through? She wasn't sure she could safely carry the dog on the back of Enbarr. She definitely couldn't carry the bear.

Wouldn't Lugh had known this logistical problem when he sent her to find his hound with his magical horse?

No way to know unless she tried. She mounted the horse and gave her a stroke. "Go home, Enbarr."

The horse neighed and pawed the ground with one foreleg. Lily held onto her silky, white mane. Clouds scudded across the light of the full moon. Lily's skin prickled in the chill.

Then it seemed the clouds descended from the sky, melding with a rolling fog, which tumbled over the surface of the ocean, coming closer and closer to them until it stopped at the edge of the beach.

She sighed. As much as she hated water, she was getting used to it now.

Together, with Failinis and the bear, they stepped onto the edge of the ocean and let the fog envelop them.

When they emerged into a brilliant, sunny day, Lily was disoriented.

Above her head, ocean waves slapped against each other. The midday sun blasted her with warm summer rays, but there was no yew forest here, nor the three mountains signaling the direction of the leprechaun's home. She couldn't even find the amazing palace where the Warrior of the Well ruled.

Instead, deep-green plains of waving grass rolled in a sharp wind. In the far distance, a shadowy line stretching across the horizon indicated a forest.

"We are in the right land, but not in the right place."

Lily spoke to no one in particular, but she knew that all the animals understood her. She thanked the gods she wasn't soaked like other times she had traveled to and from *Tir fo Thuinn*.

She sighed. "Still, I have no idea where we are."

Her eyes drooped and she yawned. She was entering a second night of no sleep and she was so tired.

Perhaps Enbarr or Failinis knew the way to their home.

She slid off the horse but kept a steadying hand on Enbarr's strong neck. "Do you know how to find Lugh?"

Enbarr pawed the ground, then trotted a few paces away, nibbling on grass.

No help there.

Lily turned to pose the same question to Failinis and heard thudding behind her. When she looked back at Enbarr, the horse was already galloping away, heading right toward the forest at the horizon.

"Wait!"

Lily ran a couple dozen paces, a futile effort. Enbarr was quicker than any other horse. She bent over, inhaling deep breaths. Both Failinis and

Cúig joined her a moment later. The bear looked bored as he plopped down on the grass, or maybe sleepy like her, too.

She eyed Failinis. "Do you know the way home?"

Before the hound could respond, a bright light exploded on the plain behind them.

Gritting her teeth and throwing an arm across her eyes, Lily tensed. *Great Mother Goddess*, what now?

When her vision cleared, her heart leapt with relief at seeing a wearied Fintan. Not that she knew the old man very well, but she had come to like his steady presence over the last few days. She had worried about leaving him behind at the High Druid's fortress.

Fintan leaned on his walking stick, a silly, toothless grin on his lined face. "Glad to see you."

She smiled. "How did you get here?"

Descended from the Tuatha Dé Danann himself, he probably had his own magic, but he hadn't shown an aptitude for creating portals to the Otherworld. *What else could he do?*

Live a long life and turn into a fish.

Fintan touched a bent finger to his nose as if reading her mind. "I had a little help from my father."

He gazed around the landscape, taking in the broad plains and distant forest. "Although I would say that some other magical being changed the course of our travels. Maybe an attempt to keep us from Lugh?" He scratched his whiskered chin, his one eye thoughtful.

Lily scratched the hound's head. "Perhaps Failinis can show us how to find Lugh."

Fintan's eye widened, and in a breathy voice, he said, "You found the leprechaun's pup!"

"I knew him all along." She grinned at the dog while stroking his neck. "He was trying to tell me the first time I met him, but I didn't recognize Lugh in his god form or remember it later when I learned who the leprechaun was."

Fintan nodded and glanced up at the ocean above their heads. "I don't recognize this part of the landscape. It's possible that Failinis might be too far from home to recognize any scents."

She groaned. "What do you say, Failinis?"

The hound put his nose to the ground and sniffed. At first, he headed behind them where the grassy plain extended beyond their line of sight. Then he turned back toward them. When he reached them, he circled them several times before stopping, then sitting in front of Lily.

"Not good," she said.

Fintan raised bushy eyebrows. "This might get hairy. I wish you could turn into a fish or a bird."

She stared at him.

Really? Was that his reaction to everything—to turn into an animal?

Then she laughed aloud, feeling it deep in her belly. She couldn't help it. They were so close to saving Rose that excitement vibrated in the veins beneath her skin, but now they were lost. She bent over, willing the laughs to stop.

Finally, she was able to draw in a deep breath, then straightened back up.

Fintan gave her a perplexed grin, a hand on one hip. "Done?"

She nodded.

He looked toward the distant forest. "This is not a land I've explored very much, although I should. My father lives here somewhere." He sighed, then looked down at the dog. "The forest?"

Enbarr had run toward the woods on the horizon. Lily ruffled Failinis's ear, and he licked her across one hand. "Better than standing here."

With a high bark and a wagging tail, Failinis took the lead, nose to ground as if he knew his home laid in the direction Fintan suggested. Lily and Fintan rushed to follow him. Cúig yawned and groaned at the same time as he lumbered to his feet to run after all of them.

They walked until the sun brightened at its peak of midafternoon, then they took a break to nibble on leftover rations in Lily's satchel and drink from a nearby stream. After getting his fill of water, Failinis left them while they ate, but quickly came back, giving a sharp bark.

Lily rolled her eyes. From the images, she knew the hound was trying more to motivate them to move rather than having found anything useful. Failinis missed his companion.

They continued their journey again. This time walking until the sun entered its twilight rotation. The forest line on the horizon grew taller until it loomed before them only twenty paces away.

Failinis halted, nose in the air toward the trees, tail sticking straight out. His whole body straightened and became rigid. Lily took his cue and peered into the forest. She saw nothing. Then she heard it. A high-pitched wail rose out of the woods.

Lily wasn't sure whether it was a woman or something unnatural. But the wail raised the hairs on her arms. It sounded forlorn, like a mother who might have lost a child.

Then the pitch changed, and fear coursed through the blood in her veins. She didn't see anything to be afraid of. It was as if the sound itself created the fear in her.

Fintan shivered. "That might not be something we want to run into."

Suddenly, Failinis shot off into the forest, a streaked hue that was quickly gone. Lily exchanged a glance with Fintan. The hound would come back. She hoped. This wasn't the first time that he had left them.

Fintan looked behind at their previous trail then glanced ahead. "Should we stop for the night here on the open plain or try walking some ways into the forest?"

Lily nibbled on her lip, remembering the dragon from last time. Sleeping on the ground here on the plain or in the forest could be a bad idea either way.

Before voicing her opinion, Fintan dropped his walking stick to gather dried twigs and grass. He brought these to where she stood. The old man must have thought sleeping on the open plain was the better plan.

Shrugging and too tired to argue, she entered the forest to crouch next to a bush for a nice sized piece of kindling when the sound of several horse hooves froze her. Half a dozen men on horseback passed right by without seeing her.

They broke free of the forest line and nearly bowled Fintan over. Cúig bounded to the old man's side, springing up onto his back legs. He growled and swiped a clawed paw, forcing the nearest horse to back away.

One rider, an older man with long, silver-blond hair and a wiry beard, circled his horse around Fintan. "Find the girl!"

The horsemen spread out, and Lily weighed her choices. She could easily back away, using her stealth to evade the men, but she couldn't abandon Fintan and Cúig. Sighing, she slapped her thigh, prepared to fight, and marched from the forest, looping her spear out of her harness and holding it before her.

"Here I am."

As she approached the older man, she noted the set of his broad shoulders, creaking leather armor, and the heavy wooden club in his large hand. A scar slashed the left side of his face, crossing from forehead to cheek. A warrior.

The man sized her up the same way she had him. His clear blue eyes widened when he sighted the harp peeking over her back. He gave a half smile. "Do you know how to use all your weapons?"

A few of his men jostled back.

Lily kept the warriors in her line of sight, but her gaze never broke from the older man, who seemed to be in charge. She swallowed against the fear worming in her middle. "Only when needed."

He nodded, raising bushy eyebrows. "Come. The Warrior of Valor requests your presence."

For the next hour, feeling she had no choice for the sake and safety of her companions, she followed the band of six men through the forest, their horses ringed around her and her group. Cúig conveyed his unease with the forest, recalling the eerie wail, but found their escort fortuitous. Lily could disagree.

No telling what the men wanted from her.

Did Lugh send them?

Perhaps he had Failinis already—the hound had not returned yet—and the nasty faery had dispatched these men to kill her, so that he wouldn't have to release Rose.

With the earthy smell of the summer forest permeating the air, she covertly perused the men. Even on horseback, they appeared to be taller than the average man back in Éire. All had varying shades of blond hair from honey to caramel in color, and each of them carried weapons and wore leather armor.

All warriors.

She would need to use the Dagda's harp to escape these men.

CHAPTER 24

"THIS WAY, GIRL." The silver-haired leader dismounted and jerked his head for Lily to follow him. The twilight sun hid behind dark clouds, casting long shadows.

The forest thinned into a rolling plain ringed by woods. In the center, rows of low, two-man tents circled one large wooden roundhouse, the roof overlaid with animal furs. One appeared to belong to a bear. A central hearth blazed before the round building, a large group of men eating, drinking, and talking around the flames. Nearby, dozens of horses whinnied in a wooden pen.

Lily hoped Cúig hadn't noticed the bear pelt, but faint images reached her, where his thoughts seemed to turn darker and less trustworthy toward the warriors. One image showed him ripping through the tents, then another one of him turning and running away. She rubbed his ear to soothe his nerves.

One tall man at the fire stood up, clapped his companion on the back, then wheeled to meet her and the silver-haired man. Even though he wore leather armor like the rest of the men, a beautiful scarlet mantle hung over his armor, fastened at his throat by a golden brooch. "Well met, Dáire. I see you've found our lost souls."

Dáire bent his head toward his superior, although it seemed more like he did it because he was supposed to, not necessarily that he saw the other man as above him. "As requested."

At this, Dáire and his men retreated to the central hearth, accepting food and drink, then recounting their small adventure.

Lily raised an eyebrow at the new man before her. *Lost souls?* She pursed her lips. "We weren't in need of rescuing."

The man looked at her. Firelight danced shadows in his light-colored eyes. He was much younger than Dáire, with the brightest blond hair hanging to his waist. Even though his boyish face was clean-shaven, he moved with the same grace as his warriors. He grasped her hand and touched a finger to his ear. She jolted at the touch and wanted to pull away, but he held her fast. "When I heard you out on the plains, I worried for your safety."

Did he mean to suggest that he himself heard us from over an hour away?

He laughed at her puzzled look.

"Please let me introduce myself." He bent his head over her hand. "I am Ardgal, the Warrior of Valor, rightful ruler of *Tír fo Thuinn*, and I have the magical gift of long-range hearing." He looked past her to Fintan. "Please enjoy my hearth and food."

Fintan gave her a smile with a wink. "He's safe." Then he eagerly found a seat among the warriors. Cúig reluctantly followed the old man, wanting food, but he kept his eyes on Lily.

She appreciated his concern.

Lily frowned back at Ardgal and tried once more to pull her hand from his, but he smoothly grasped her hand in both of his and pulled her to him. He placed her pale hand on his chest.

Cúig growled low in his throat, but Ardgal ignored the bear. A smile played on his pink lips. "I feared for your safety in the forest, and when it was clear that you planned to camp with just an old man and a bear who doesn't know how to use his claws, I knew that we should rescue you."

Being near him, with his breath on her cheek, she could see that his blue eyes were like the stars after a wet mist. Her heart thudded against her chest. She'd never been this close to a man before, except for those related to her. "You don't plan to harm us?"

He feigned a wounded look. "I am a but a man who helps anyone who needs it. Easier done when I haven't been ousted by my own brother. He resides in my place at the palace, allowing wild and dangerous creatures free to roam the forests. So, I've sworn to protect my citizens until I can gain my throne again."

He looked over his shoulder and whistled. A woof responded to him, and Lily's eyes grew wide as Failinis shot out of the large central roundhouse. This time, the warrior released her hand so that she could kneel and throw her arms around Failinis. "I knew you wouldn't abandoned us, you silly hound!"

Awkwardly, she stood, not wanting to offend the man, but she wasn't sure they should trust him. "Why did your men treat us like prisoners with no choice? They could have just as easily invited us to stay this evening with you."

"They shouldn't have reacted that way." Ardgal narrowed his eyes on his men, then on Dáire. "Perhaps they were trying to be careful in case you should be dangerous."

"A woman, an old man, and a bear?"

He laughed at his words being thrown back at him, then winked. "Can't be too careful. Old men can be dangerous." Again, he shot a look at Dáire, one that spoke of a future meeting between the two of them.

Dáire shrugged. "She has the Dagda's harp."

The Warrior of Valor's mouth dropped open in surprise. Then they narrowed on the harp just peeking over her shoulder. His voice was filled with awe. "You've been to the leprechaun's home."

She thought carefully about her words, wondering what she should reveal to this stranger. She decided to be truthful. Perhaps the man could help them as he said. "We search for him." Her voice was rusty again, so it came out low. The man leaned closer to hear her, and her body tensed. If he could hear so well, then he didn't need to be so near her, unless he was intent on taking the harp.

Seeing her reaction, he straightened. "Do I scare you?"

Did he? She didn't think so, but then the way he looked at her, like a starving rat with a fallen piece of bread, made her uncomfortable. "I've learned not to trust strangers."

Ardgal ran a hand over his mouth, his fingers sliding over his clean-shaven chin. "It's a hard way to live, always expecting the worst."

"Better to be realistic." She glanced around at the group of men making a life in the forest, a place filled with fearful beings and magical creatures. Fintan seemed completely at ease in that group, adding to their stories. Then she turned her attention back to Ardgal. "If you had been realistic, would you have lost your throne?"

The man laughed out loud and slapped her on the back of her shoulder, jerking her whole body forward. "Maybe I should keep you for counsel."

Lily shook her head, her brows drawing down. Is this when he would spring his trap and capture them as prisoners? "I have other priorities."

He wiped a tear from his eye. "No worries. I jest, but I like your point of view."

Ardgal gripped her hand again, drawing her toward the fire and helping her find a seat next to him. A soldier handed over wooden bowls of sweet-smelling stew. Ardgal's mirth settled with the first aromatic bite. Around a piece of potato, he asked, "Do these priorities bring you to our lands?"

Lily settled with the food, Failinis lying at her feet. Belly full, Cúig stretched out behind her, rolling in the grass. "I'm here to rescue my sister."

Ardgal rubbed a dribble of stew from his mouth. "The leprechaun?"

Failinis raised his head to look between the two of them. Then he huffed and rested his head on the ground again, eyes closing.

Lily nodded. "He has her."

"Tomorrow, I will help you find the leprechaun's home. It's less than a day's ride from here." In the firelight, she saw Ardgal become quiet, his eyes thoughtful as he studied her. She found herself unable to eat with his stare, but then he broke the long silence. "Forgive me, but you look like one of the people, yet you are unfamiliar. Which land do you come from?"

She furrowed her brow, having no idea what he meant.

Fintan cleared his throat from several paces away, drawing their attention. "Warrior of Valor, please let me introduce us. I am Fintan mac Bóchra. This is Líle níc Muaich from Éire of the green plains."

Ardgal choked on his food, then took a swallow of his waterskin. Red flushed his cheeks when he faced her again. "Forgive my confusion, lady, but how did you come to our world then?"

Lily shifted through the answers she could give but decided on the truth again. She opened her mouth to respond, but suddenly, the high-pitched wail ripped through the campsite. It was piercingly higher than before.

Throwing hands over her ears, Lily squeezed her eyes shut. She had almost forgotten about the earlier wail. This one echoed throughout the forest for long minutes. No one could escape the sound or the feelings it produced—sadness, longing, despair.

Then it was gone.

Lily shivered.

"The Lady in White," Ardgal said.

Fintan scooted closer to them. "The Lady in White? I have never heard of her."

The warrior leader shook his head, firelight catching in his blond strands, streaking white lines through them. "Only a few months has she been here, but they say she mourns the loss of her family." He pointed to the east. "My brother keeps her prisoner in the palace. If I was to get my throne back, my first act would be to release her."

Dáire spat into the fire, producing a hissing sound. "Conall saw her once. Said she was very beautiful."

Ardgal shook his head. "She could be a hag, for all I care. No creature deserves the pain we hear in her sorrows. I would free her of that if I could."

Lily swallowed the bite of carrot in her mouth. "Why is she called the Lady in White?"

"Easy enough." Dáire rubbed the scar on his cheek with an absent finger. "Everyone who sees her says that she's always wearing white." The older man chuckled. "She's also very pale from all the crying she does."

The men's voices then raised over each other, everyone trying to pitch his voice to be heard over their companion with some story about the Lady in White. But then Ardgal stood, and the voices hushed. Lily pondered whether they did it out of respect or fear. But as the warrior leader spoke, she saw devotion shining in the eyes of the men around her. They truly liked him.

He raised a hand. "The night is drawing to an end. See to the old man's accommodations. I will take care of our young lady." He held a hand down to Lily.

She swallowed her stew. She wasn't sure she liked his words. Did he expect something of her? However, a part of her was grateful. She hadn't slept in two days.

Failinis looked at her, his eyes glossy in the firelight. She wished the hound could tell her something about the man. He had found the Warrior of Valor, after all. Perhaps that was all she needed to know. Putting the wooden bowl aside and wiping her hands on her trousers, she accepted his offered hand, and he pulled her up.

Cúig rose with a hum deep in his throat. He came to her side as if to follow wherever she may go.

Ardgal looked into the bear's eyes. "I'm sorry, my friend, but you will need to sleep outside with my men, unless you're a prince in a bear's body?"

Cúig moaned but turned away.

The Warrior of Valor gave a final wave and one last smile to his men. "I will see you all in the morning, my friends."

A few hollers and whoops followed them into the large roundhouse, making Lily frown. She ducked past the leather doorway and found herself in a near-dark room. Within moments, Ardgal had lit a short candle, revealing a small space divided by a wall of white linen. The floor was completely covered in soft animal skins.

"This is the beginning of my new kingdom." His back was to her as he lit more candles around the room. "This roundhouse will be a workshop. Soon, I will have a brand-new palace, standing back along the woods."

He turned to her after lighting the last candle, which he handed over. He noted her frown. "Ignore my men." He swept back some of his hair, which was so close in color to her own in this light. "I have a reputation where women are concerned, but truthfully, I never expect it."

Heat flamed across Lily's cheeks, and she looked down at her feet.

The man's eyes widened. "You've never known a man?"

Lily choked on the words she meant to say. Her cough almost blew out the candle. After recovering, her face pinker than before, she shook her head.

"You'll not know your first from me, although I'd wish it otherwise." His fingers traced the outline of her cheek. "You are a beautiful woman."

Lily feared that his statement would be proved untrue if he kept looking at her and touching her the way he did now. She stepped away from his fingers.

His hand lingered in the air for a moment, then he sighed.

"I would never take anything from you that you were not willing to give of your own free will." He pointed to a spot in the linen divider, where Lily could make out a faint rumple in the fabric. "Through there you will find my pallet. I may not have my brother's magical gift of heightened smell, but I will sleep out here and dream of the day I claim my bed again and smell your sweet scent upon the blankets."

Quickly, Lily fumbled through the opening to the back half of the roundhouse and ducked inside. For a moment, she breathed a sigh of relief. The emotions that tumbled through her body confused her, but she knew she was grateful for not spending the night in the same bed as the man just a few feet from her.

"I hear your stilted breathing, Líle níc Muaich of the green plains. Please be rest assured that I will not allow any harm to come to you."

Lily winced. She'd momentarily forgotten about his magical gift of long-range hearing.

She unlaced her leather shoes, stretching her toes in the soft animal skins, and dropped her satchel on the ground. She grasped both her spear and the harp before blowing out the candle and making her way to a raised box that served as his pallet. His bed was soft.

Then she remembered his words about smelling her when she was gone and sniffed the blanket. She nearly blanched. It smelled like a man in need of a bath, one who had been working out in the hot sun for several days.

She silently gagged before tucking the harp underneath the blanket. She wedged it between her legs. The spear she kept a firm hold of, resting it on her chest outside the blanket.

Tomorrow she would rescue Rose.

Tomorrow she would be reunited with her sister.

Sniffing the blanket again, Lily wondered if the man's stink would rub off on her.

CHAPTER 25

A HAND ON LILY'S shoulder dragged her out of her deep slumber, and she automatically raised the spear. When sleep finally cleared her eyes, she realized that the Warrior of Valor had simply tried to wake her, but now he held very still, the sharp tip of the spear pressing against his throat.

"Good morning." He didn't seem at all fazed by the weapon as he smiled down at her.

Quickly, she pulled the spear away. "I apologize."

He stepped back. "No need. This will be one visit I'll never forget." He rubbed a hand across his neck. "When you're ready, we should be able to guide you in the right direction."

When she nodded, he ducked out of the room.

Lily lay back for a moment, gathering her thoughts.

Then elation ran from her heart up her throat. Today, she would save Rose, and she would have her sister back. Not wasting another moment, she jumped from the pallet box, tied on her shoes, and strapped her harp and spear into the harness.

Outside, the camp was alive under a full morning sun. Horses were being fed. Several men lugged wooden containers of water from the wood line. Another dumped waste from a cookpot. Others sharpened swords or spear points.

Ardgal sat astride a horse, waiting on her. He leaned down to offer a hand, which she felt she couldn't deny, so she loosened her spear to hold, and then grasped his hand. In a swift, easy motion, he pulled her up in front of him. Then, in a movement of familiarity, he slid an arm around her and pulled her firmly against him.

A few of his men cheered, and Lily's face grew hot, first with embarrassment, then anger. This time her reputation wouldn't suffer, knowing what insinuations were being perpetuated. She threw a sharp elbow into his stomach. He groaned and released his tight hold. The same men who cheered now shared a laugh.

"Well done," he said, low enough only for her as he guided his horse using his knees. He pointed the beast farther into the forest line, heading east.

Lily was ready to voice her concerns about leaving her friends, when she saw Fintan trotting up on a borrowed horse, with both Cúig and Failinis loping a few paces behind. A few other warriors joined their party, but they stayed behind their leader.

Over her shoulder, Lily frowned. "Why couldn't I have my own horse?"

Ardgal leaned close to her ear so that his breath tickled her cheek. "Did you not enjoy setting the record straight about what happened in the roundhouse last night?"

She widened her eyes. Did the man purposefully set up this morning's display to save her reputation or was that only a byproduct that he now claimed credit for?

She didn't have faith in him to answer her truthfully so held her tongue.

A bright sun shot shafts of light through the canopy of trees. Birdsong twittered among the high branches. The sweet smell of flowers and berries mingled with fresh grass.

Everything reminded Lily of summer.

Summer was when they lost Marigold.

But she wouldn't lose Rose today.

At midday, they stopped for less than half an hour, resting the horses, filling waterskins, and eating dried fish. Then they mounted and rode through the forest again. Two hours later, the forest ended in a new plain. In the distance, the familiar palace twinkled. A circle of pillar stones ringed the well, cresting a large hill. To the east, the forest of red yew trees shook their branches with a quick wind.

The Warrior of Valor dismounted, helping her slide from the horse's back. This time his hands were only helpful and not overly friendly. "It was a pleasure spending the night with you. Please remember me more fondly than you might."

Lily smoothed down her tunic before pitching her voice low, knowing he would be the only one to hear. "Ever try anything like this morning again and you'll never worry about another woman who couldn't think of you fondly."

The warrior threw back his head and laughed a mighty roar. As his merriment died away, he ran a hand through his long blond hair. "You have brightened my week. I wish you the best of luck in your quest to save your sister."

Lily nodded, swallowing. The man surprised her yet again. In her experience, most men didn't like threats, so his laughter confused her. "Good luck in recapturing your throne."

He bowed his head with a smile, then mounted his horse. He tilted his head toward the distant palace before looking at her again. "I'm sorry I cannot help you any further." He touched one of his ears. "I don't hear my brother moving yet, but if he knew I was this close, he would send a storm our way. Soon, he's likely to smell my presence here."

Ardgal sniffed then gave a hand signal to his men, and almost as one, the entire party turned in a wide U-shape to slide away into the forest once more.

Lily didn't wait to see the warriors leave. Her whole body hummed with energy, preparing for the confrontation with Lugh. After she took several strides toward the red forest, Failinis sprinted ahead of her, barking as if calling out to his beloved immortal. Cúig gave a low-volume grunt as he lumbered next to her, bringing his scent of musk and berries. Fintan shadowed them, his walking stick striking the ground in an even gait.

This time, the forest did not have them walking in circles. The path remained continuous, with the hound leading the way. In less than two hours, they had reached Lugh the leprechaun's home. Failinis sat at the door, wagging his tail quick along the ground, his head swiveling from Lily to the door and back again, as if telling her that she was taking too long to catch up.

At the glass entrance, she paused, looking down at the dog. "Please let me enter first."

Failinis stepped back.

Not waiting a moment more, she slapped her thigh in preparation for a possible fight, then pulled on the metal knob and marched down the glass hallway.

She held the harp ready in her hands, taking each step purposely until coming to the cavernous cave in the side of the mountain. Rose was there, chained to the wall again. The eagle hopped along the ground in front of her, chasing a cricket and causing her to laugh so that she didn't see Lily.

The little man had been watching Rose with a silly grin on his craggy face, but he caught Lily's entrance right away. Fintan and the bear followed behind her, with Failinis no longer able to contain himself as he bounded inside with a great woof, his tail whipping the air.

"My hound!" The small man fell over when the dog jumped on him with two forepaws, licking his face all over.

Lily waited only a few moments before speaking up, but she hardened her voice against its usual hoarseness. "Release my sister."

The leprechaun pushed Failinis aside to come back to his feet. He wiped slobber from his face. "I have more riches than you can amass in your lifetime. Would you take them in return for bringing back my hound?"

"I want my sister." She held up the harp, ready to play, but Fintan put a hand on her arm.

"You can't banish me this time, Lugh," he said. "You must come back home. Your sister is worried about you. Ébliu will not stop pestering me."

"You stupid oaf! Why get married?" Lugh tugged his gray beard. "My sister won't leave you alone? Fine. We'll fix that." With a wiggle of his beard, he sent Fintan crashing past the entrance to tumble further back into the cave.

The sound of a grumbled roar sent chills through Lily. *What monster hid back there?*

"No pestering from Ébliu anymore." Lugh laughed and yelled his words at the back of the cave. "Just watch out for the dragon!"

Suddenly, the bear roared forward, thinking to take advantage of the little man's distraction. Lugh swung around and fluttered his fingers, his beard turning golden in a bright light. Cúig stopped in mid-leap. His paws ran in the air but made no progress.

"And you, my friend, wouldn't be in your predicament if you hadn't looked for my gold. For that," Lugh wagged a finger back and forth, "you can go look at all the gold you want but no touching or the dragon will get you."

Cúig flew back into the cave's darkness, disappearing the same way Fintan had been dismissed.

Lily shook, her teeth ground so tightly together that she lost feeling in her jaw. She strummed the first chord of the sleeping song.

The leprechaun held up a hand. "Come *Daur da Bláo*, apple-sweet murmurer, come, *Coir Cethair Chuir*, four-angled frame of harmony, come summer, come winter, out of the mouths of harps and bags and pipes!"

The harp flew from her hands to his, ripped right out of her grasp. Only a second passed before she pulled out her spear, ready to hurtle the iron tip through him, but then she was blinded by a bright light. She blinked several times to clear away the spots in her eyes.

When she could see again, she was back home.

Right outside the wooden palisade of *Ráth Bláthanna*.

CHAPTER 26

LILY PULLED THE FUR blanket back over her head, hiding her wet face. She pretended that it smelled of musk and berries like her friend, Cúig. In reality, not one of their furs came from bears because none had existed for over a thousand years.

"Lily!" Ciara's voice came loud enough through the blanket. "You cannot spend the rest of your life like this. It's been four days."

That meant it had been nearly two weeks since she had lost Rose for good.

Lily grunted in reply, squeezing her closed eyes tighter. Her eyelids were hot and puffy. Her chest continually ached. *Hadn't I imagined this reality once before?* No Marigold. No Rose.

Add Cúig to the list of loss.

She pressed fingers to her mouth to hold back a sob. She didn't know how to live life anymore. Everything hurt so much.

"You are to be married to Dermot in a few days."

Ciara didn't want to force her to get married, but what else could her mother do? The *taoiseach* had ordered Lily's marriage to her cousin. With Rose gone, the chief seemed to think it even more important that clan ties be solidified.

Tears squeezed between her crusted eyelids. Her shoulders shook as she withheld screams of pain racking deep within her body.

How could Rose be gone forever?

It was so unfair.

Rose alive in another world, but so far away, a prisoner to a monster. Lily ached all over. She cried for her sister who might never know peace again.

Would I ever see my sister again in this lifetime?

First Marigold, now Rose.

It was all her fault. She should have been more careful. She should have stopped Marigold from diving into the ocean. She should have stopped Rose from approaching the despicable leprechaun. The faery could not be trusted. Her sisters were the core of her world. She remembered their laughter, their unconditional love for her.

She loved them and missed them so much.

Please let Rose come home.

Her pleading echoed in her mind.

A headache pounded harshly against the inside of her skull, and even though the pain halted the steady trail of tears, the minute she wiped her nose and tried to breathe, the tears started again.

The pounding resumed but increased in intensity.

She hit her palm against her forehead.

Living was too painful.

If only she'd been a better sister, she wouldn't have lost the people she cared about the most. And Cúig, poor Cúig, who had comforted her so many times over the last few days. Her friend and companion.

He was lost to her.

She moaned, hot tears salty on her tongue.

If only she had told the bear to stay behind. He hadn't needed to go with her. Now he was a prisoner of the leprechaun, unable to roll in the grass like he was wont to do.

She was such an awful person for allowing him to be captured and probably eaten by the dragon. It was a death too horrible to think about.

If only she could make it back to the Otherworld. She'd trade herself for all of them or join them, just so that she wouldn't be alone or feel so miserable for being the only one left.

If only she could make it back, she'd rescue Rose.

A hand rubbed her shoulder through the blanket, and she stiffened.

Her mother must have been standing there the whole time. Now Ciara did what she could to comfort her.

Lily had to remind herself that others loved her. Her mother. Nana. They loved and accepted her faults.

Even if my mamaí had faults, too.

She keened. What had her mother been thinking? Violently, she shook her head. No. Her mamaí was only guilty of loving the wrong person.

Like how her sisters had loved and trusted Lily. They had always loved her no matter her follies, but now it was her fault they were gone.

She yelled in her mind.

I miss you both so much!

Sobs knocked against her chest, and they escaped through her open mouth, a desperate bawl. She gulped for breath.

The pressure from Ciara's hand increased. "It's all right, Lily. Let it out."

Beneath her covers, she shook her head and bit down on her closed fist to stop any other sound.

Then she felt her mother move away. "I'm here when you need me." Her words sounded small and sad.

Lily realized that her mother probably hurt as much as she did, maybe more because she had lost her daughters, children who should have been with her as she aged and passed from this world.

Ciara had lost two children. And now her lover.

Lily felt selfish. Despair scented the stale air. Her tears dried suddenly. What could she do?

Something. Something.

She had to do something. Her anguish weakened. A pinpoint of determined focus grew in her mind. She'd just have to find a way to the Otherworld.

But how? Hadn't she thought of this as soon as she returned?

She couldn't ask for help from the *Ard-Draoi*, because she had barged in on his dinner and had ruined all of it.

In desperation, perhaps she should try the High Druid. But he'd likely kill her.

Wouldn't that be better? a small part of her mind asked.

She had also stolen Failinis from Hera. Even if the dog wasn't Hera's, Lily had broken the hospitality laws.

Ana... *Not really Ana!*

She might have been able to help Lily, but the woman had disappeared after Lily confronted her on first returning from *Tír fo Thuinn.*

When Lily had stepped through the ráth gates, Ana and Ciara stood side by side, staring at Lily as she walked toward them. Her mother's eyes had slid past her, looking for Rose.

The weight of Rose's loss had nearly broken Lily in that moment; then she met Ana's steely gaze. Her dry mouth and heavy feet were forgotten. Her nostrils flared and she had stomped over to the *bandraoi.* "How dare you!"

Ana's lips pinched, and she grasped her own wrist with the opposite hand, her shoulders rounded forward. She opened her mouth, but Lily cut her off.

"You are a pretender." She jerked her head, and her voice shook. "All this time, you probably had the magic to rescue Rose yourself, yet you sit here, doing what?"

Ana stood straighter, shaking her head. "You don't understand..."

"Should I pretend that I care?" Her rushing heartbeat pounded in her ears. She withdrew her spear from the halter without even realizing what she was doing.

Ciara jumped between them, holding up a hand to Lily. "Let's hear what she has to say."

She pointed the spear tip toward Ana. "That woman has lied to us for years." She glared down at her mother. "Do you know she has powerful magic?"

Before Ciara could respond, Ana gently brushed the shorter woman aside and walked into the spear tip so that it pierced the top of her wool cloak. A quick wind shuffled through the *lis*. Clouds scurried over the sun, darkening everything into twilight. Ana returned Lily's resistant stare with her own, swallowing hard. "I have reasons for what I must do."

Then she raised her arms, her wrists limp, and the wind rushed toward her. The very darkness in the sky funneled down and touched Ana.

Lily nearly fell to her feet to back away but then the wind threatened to knock her over. Several others who had been watching the exchange did fall. Lily planted the butt-end of her spear in the ground and held on with both hands, her hair whipping all around.

Just as suddenly as the wind and shadows had come, it had all faded away. Where Ana had stood, a different woman stared at Lily. The sun highlighted the younger woman, painting streaks through long, black hair, glinting off rowanberry-red lips. In place of Ana's brown linen dress over a tan tunic, she now wore a long, midnight-colored dress with delicate silver embroidery hinted in the curves of the deep neckline and wrists.

Lily gasped. She recognized the stranger from the leprechaun's cave home. Then she remembered that the woman had been familiar to her even then as now. The woman had Ana's upturned nose and deep brown, nearly black eyes, but the *bandraoi* had never worn any coloring on her lips.

She took a cautious step backward. "Ana?"

"That is one of my old names."

The voice was the same. *How hadn't I heard that before?*

"I am the Morrígan."

The *Ard-Draoi*'s words came back to Lily: The goddess reveals herself. How hadn't Lily realized the implication before?

Standing there, dumbfounded, Lily couldn't find her voice until Ciara rejoined them after having been one of the ones who had fallen. She placed a hand on Mórrígan's arm, and the two women exchanged a glance that spoke of a long friendship, love, and trust.

Lily covered her heart with a shaky hand, feeling a deep ache there, and drew her brows together. "Mother, you knew?"

Ciara would have spoken but Mórrígan touched pale fingertips to Ciara's hand. "I have done what has needed to be done. Do not blame your mother for that."

Lily grit her teeth. "You've allowed Rose to suffer as the leprechaun's prisoner. You would see her die!"

In a second almost too quick for Lily to see it, the woman's chin trembled, then a dull, glazed look replaced the immobility in her dark-colored eyes. "What would you have me do?"

"Save my sister."

"I can't."

"Then open a portal for me."

The Morrígan shook her head.

Lily whipped the spear around to point the way out of the *ráth*. "Then leave and never come back."

Later, she would wonder where she had gained the courage to speak such a way to an immortal goddess, but at that moment she was too enraged to logically think through her actions.

Mórrígan's facial features sagged, making her look older, a little more like Ana. The goddess turned woodenly to Ciara, grasping her hands. Her voice was flat when she spoke. "I think it's best I stay away."

Ciara nodded, tears brimming in her eyes. "I appreciate the time we've had. I will always have a great love for you."

Shock still hummed in Lily's mind. Her mother had known something about who Ana had really been, yet she had never said anything. The women seemed to have forgotten she stood there as they hugged each other. Then Ana's pale hands cupped Ciara's face and the two kissed in a way that brimmed with more passion than any Lily had seen shared between them.

Ana broke the kiss, straightening away from Ciara with a longing look. Then, with her shoulders back and chin notched up, she stepped toward the wooden gates of the *ráth*. The gate groaned open of its own accord. Never looking back, Ana walked through the arch, her last stride dissolving as her body broke into a dozen ravens that wheeled skyward with loud squawks.

Ana—Mórrígan—hadn't been seen since that day.

A small part of Lily felt awful for dismissing Mórrígan. As Ana, she had been a steady figure all her life and at the various *ráth*s. Her absence was felt by all in the settlement from that day forward. But Ana had lied to them, hiding that she was a real and breathing goddess. And that same goddess refused to help save Rose. Anger stirred deep in Lily's breast.

That anger leaked over to her mother.

Lily had never received an explanation of what her mother had really known. Then anger had melted into despair.

It had been easy to believe that the good folk and the Great Mother Goddess had never existed when she had lost Marigold in the ocean, but to know now that they were all real and none helped Marigold and none would help Rose, Lily wanted to forsake them all.

She rolled over to her side in the pallet, shuffling down into the blanket, ready to let sleep drag her into the abyss, pretend that she could die, when she felt something digging into her hip. She reached in for the offending object, and when her fingers closed around it, her heart skipped a beat before pounding rapidly.

It was Hera's coin.

She had forgotten about it all this time.

Could Hera help her?

She blew out through her lips. *Only if the woman didn't realize that I had been the one to take her dog.*

Not really hers, though.

Not really a woman, either.

Another goddess.

Lily mulled that over. Over the last few days, she had come to accept that everything supernatural was indeed possible. Mórrígan was really a goddess associated with war, death, and fate. Lugh the leprechaun was really the god of skill and mastery, oaths, truth, and the law, connected with light, storms, and the sun. Other realms existed.

If Éire's legends were truths, couldn't other lands also have real legends?

There was also whatever had happened between Mórrígan and Hera. The two women seemed to have a history, loathing each other, yet both were powerful. Hera had to be a goddess, too.

A goddess who might be able to help her save Rose.

Hadn't Hera told her to call if she ever needed help?

May the Mother Goddess keep me from harm. But then, what had the Mother Goddess ever done for her?

With a new plan invigorating her for the first time in days, she rolled from the pallet. A pungent smell assailed her, nearly knocking her back into the fur blankets.

Maybe she should bathe first.

CHAPTER 27

"NO, PAISTE, YOU CAN'T EAT the old man or the bear! Not yet!"

The dragon's grunt in response rumbled out to the cave's main entrance. "Can't rest with all this good meat around."

Lugh heard the dragon's scales scrape along the floor as he exited through one of the tunnels at the very back of the cave.

"Why leave them back there?" Mousie stared at him when he looked up from the fidchell game. No longer chained and back in her original form, she sat on the rocky cave floor across from him, with the game between them on a small tree stump. Her eagle, never far from her, twitched his head from side to side, looking at the gold and silver pieces on the square wooden board. The board itself was made of wood, but the edges and corners were trimmed in gold and inlaid with jewels.

"Make a move, Mousie."

"I don't understand this game." Her fingers twirled red curls as she studied the board.

"Just move one!"

Her wide blue eyes peeked up at him. "Could you show me another move?"

With an impatient snort, he walked over to her side and glanced across the board. He pointed at one of her silver pieces. "See there, my pair of gold men are almost on the same line as your man, which will stop you from crossing."

He looked at her to see if she understood. Her face was close to his. Her hair tickled his cheek.

Strawberries.

It was a delightful smell.

But strawberries?

He swiped at her hair, yanking a fist through curls and pulling several strands free.

She yelped and fell back. Her pale face turned up to his, eyes wide but brow furrowed. She blinked several times.

"I shouldn't have..." His voice cracked. Then he raised his chin. When had he decided he wouldn't kill her anymore? He couldn't remember. "Where did you get scented soaps to bathe with?"

He had specifically given her soap made of bark when he took her down to the river to bathe that morning. But he didn't watch her as she undressed and waded into the water.

"A-a... f-faery... wo—"

"Spit it out of that useless hole in your face." He slapped a hand on the fidchell board, and it crashed to the ground.

The lines on Mousie's face tightened. "Make up your mind!" she yelled as she climbed to her feet.

"Huh?"

Mousie stomped over to her place against the wall and stood over the chains. "One minute, you save me from a monstrous man and care for my wounds as if you're my lover, and in the next, you are the same monstrous man who inflicted my wounds."

"You are mine, not his." A hard stitch hit his chest as he said the words, but he brushed it off.

She crossed her arms. "I have done everything you've asked of me. I haven't tried to escape, not even when you sent my sister away twice."

"You wouldn't be able to escape." He sneered.

"Do you really have so little compassion?" Her bottom lip quivered. "I'm here without family, living with your cruel tortures."

"What do I have to be compassionate about? I have no family."

"I always believed that there was a good man inside you, Lugh, because I believe I know what you've lost."

How could she have ever had so much faith in him? Surely, she could see she was wrong. "Don't say my name."

She tilted her head. "You lost a son, Lugh. You lost who you were supposed to be. You need to face your reality."

He balled his fists and raised one toward her.

Mousie snorted. "I see now that I have been delusional. How can you be the great demigod when you don't even keep your promises?" She reached over and snapped the chains onto her own ankle, and then laid down on the floor, her back to him.

His vision turned white, then red. Anger boiled deep within his chest, threatening to burst and burn his whole house down.

He changed his mind. He would kill her right now.

He raised his hands, a glow emanating from his gray beard. He'd make it painful. Sparks jumped between his fingers.

Then her shoulders trembled, and she buried her head in her arms, a soft sob escaping. His limbs weakened, and he dropped his arms. They felt like stone blocks thrown into a lake. He wanted to rush to her and...

And what?

He couldn't remember what to do.

So, he decided to go fishing.

CHAPTER 28

LOOKING FOR SOLITUDE after she finished her wash and telling no one of her plan, Lily hiked to *An Abhainn Bradán*, the Salmon River, following its winding path for several miles, spear strapped on her back. With most of the afternoon gone, she finally stopped at the river's edge. She knelt on both knees and dipped her fingers into the cool water, watching tiny fish scatter.

Marigold could talk to them if she were here.

With that thought, Lily peered around, hoping to see her ghostly sister. *Marigold, guide me!*

She closed her eyes and reached out with her mind's awareness. The images of dozens of woodland creatures entered her consciousness. She connected briefly with each one, taking slow, deep breaths in through her nose and out through her mouth. It soothed her to communicate with animals. The mental images grounded her like nothing else.

When she felt ready, she withdrew the gold coin with a woman's likeness on the surface. She quirked her mouth. It was probably Hera's likeness. Then, she held it out in her open palm.

"Hera."

Nothing happened at first except the forest seemed to take a pause in its breath of life. Then the air shimmered only a few paces away. A blinding light cast across her eyes.

Did every god and goddess use bright light?

She squeezed her eyes tight to preserve her vision. When dancing light spots disappeared from her eyesight, she saw the beautiful woman standing before her. Hera looked down upon her, frowning, her back straight. The gold crown in her dark hair gleamed in a shaft of sunlight.

It seemed the goddess controlled the very rays of the sun.

During her bath and subsequent walk, Lily had thought for a long time about what she would say and ask. She didn't want to waste her breath on things that didn't matter, and she certainly didn't want to waste this magical woman's time. No telling what she'd do.

Staying in her kneeling position with the hope of showing supplication, Lily cleared her throat, and discreetly pocketed the gold coin. This trick may not work again, but she'd take the chance again if needed. "Can you help me rescue my sister?"

Hera tilted her head, a curl brushing her cheek at the motion. The peacock feather waved trailing fingers along her head. "It was a curious happenstance that when you disappeared from the High Druid's fortress that my dog was gone, too."

Lily kept herself from wincing, not wanting to give herself away. "When I woke up, all I could think about was leaving. I didn't see Jason." She showed her palms. "I didn't know I traveled in the company of a dangerous goddess. Perhaps she took Jason."

Hera scowled. "Troublesome woman."

Her reaction was what Lily had hoped for to throw suspicion off herself. She swallowed, allowing tears to cloud her eyes. "Please, Hera. Help me bring my sister home."

The goddess's brows pulled in and she stroked a gloved thumb across Lily's cheek. "Where is she?"

"In the Otherworld, *Tír fo Thuinn.*"

Hera pulled her hand away, the corners of her mouth turning down. "The Otherworld is not part of my domain. I cannot enter without the permission of a Tuatha Dé Danann or other being of the land." Her slender fingers rubbed the fabric of her luxurious cloak, her look pensive. "I may be able to open a portal to allow you to enter but rescuing your sister and returning to this world will be up to you."

Twice Lily had come up against the little man. Twice she had lost. She had hoped to have the help of someone just as powerful or more powerful than Lugh, so she was disappointed that Hera couldn't go with her. Regardless, she wasn't willing to pass up on the chance to go back to the Otherworld. She had another plan, and if her plan didn't work, at least she would be closer to Rose. Or she would die trying.

She nodded.

"You must do a favor for me in return."

Lily wasn't sure what the goddess would want from her, a mere mortal, but nodded again after swallowing hard.

Hera smiled. "The *Ard-Draoi* of your land told me that I can find my lost eagle in the Otherworld. I believe that he may be with Lugh the leprechaun." Her fingers clenched at the fabric of her cloak. "Rescue him. Bring my beloved pet back to me. I miss him dearly."

Lily remembered the eagle. He had always been with Rose. Since Rose could speak to sky creatures, it shouldn't be hard to convince the eagle to come back with her if Lily was able to free her and find a way back home. "What if I don't make it back?"

Hera waved a hand, gold bracelets jangling on her wrist. "No worries, then, but if you do return to this land, ensure you have my eagle, because I will hunt you down if you don't have him."

The blood drained from Lily's face, her breathing suddenly shallow. She didn't doubt the goddess could hurt her or worse. "I swear by the gods of my lands that I will rescue my sister and your eagle. I will bring both home or die trying."

That satisfied Hera, and a beautiful smile lit up her face. She flicked her wrist, and the air in the space next to her shimmered.

Lily barely hesitated, only looking once at Hera before leaping into the shimmer.

CHAPTER 29

ON THE OTHER SIDE, warmth hit her in the face. The sun was at the top of its day. A sense of determination filled her, because she had a plan for when she saw the leprechaun again. For days during her crying, she had thought about how things could have played out differently the last time she was in the little man's home.

Lugh was a god associated with many things. That was her key.

She stood with the red yew tree forest behind her, facing the glass façade of the leprechaun's house. She snuck a peek around for a glimpse of Enbarr, but the white horse was nowhere to be found.

She wrung her hands, feeling their clamminess. A bit of disappointment and dread mixed together. If she was successful in saving Rose, how would they get home?

Perhaps they could find the Warrior of Valor, and he would know a way to help them. And if he didn't, perhaps they could travel with Ardgal and his men until they found a way. It wouldn't matter how long that would take as long as she was with her sister again.

But then she cringed, thinking of her mother and grandmother. They would believe the worst had happened to them, not even knowing that Lily had gone back to *Tir fo Thuinn*.

She shook her head to put aside thoughts that would only slow her down, then braided her hair back. She left her spear in its strap on her back. Experience had taught her that she couldn't win with physical force or with a weapon. She had to use her mind against Lugh.

Digging the nails of one hand into the other, she found the courage to move and stride up to the strange glass door with the metal knob. She slapped her thigh for the coming confrontation.

The house was strange, but then she had seen and experienced so many strange things in the last couple of weeks that they all almost seemed commonplace now.

The door readily slid out, and she marched down the glass hallway. Her footfalls echoed, but she didn't try to hide her entrance. When she came to the spacious cave room at the end of the hallway, she stopped.

Rose stood to the far-right wall, with her ankle chained and the eagle on her arm. Failinis lay on the stone floor, his tail thumping when he saw her.

Lugh stirred something in a huge cauldron over the central hearth, his back to Lily's approach. He banged his wooden spoon on the metal lip. "So, you've come back? Do you wish for me to simply put you out of your misery?"

Lily wanted to flinch, but her resolve kept her steady. She squared her shoulders back.

The little man turned around. At first, a frown pulled at the deep lines of his face, then his mouth opened in a slow "O."

"Perhaps you want something else?" he asked.

"You will release my sister to me, Lugh Lámfada."

He snorted. "You think to name me?"

Rose shuffled a foot forward, the chains clinking on the rocky ground. "You are a great god, Lugh."

His face brightened red. When he spoke, his voice took on a hard edge and spittle dripped into his beard. "Do not assume you know me, Mousie."

Lily frowned. "But I know you." And some distant memory of this man as a golden god rose to the surface of her consciousness, making her statement feel like a truth in fact. "You are the God of the Sun, the God of Crafts, the God of the Arts, the God of Storms... "

"You don't know what you speak of." Lugh balled his fists as he stalked toward her.

Lily raised her chin. "You are the God of Oaths."

Lugh stopped.

He waved a hand, which made Lily tense. She had seen that hand wave too many times and the end results, but he didn't banish her back to her home.

Instead, he made a pfft sound. "I can lie as much as I want."

Rose lifted a hand, holding it out to him in a plea. "But that is not the man I've come to know, Lugh."

He threw her a dark look. "Stop saying my name!"

"Lugh." Rose dropped to her knees, the eagle hopping to the ground, her chains rustling. "You are a wonderful man, capable of so much more. Please remember."

While focused on her sister and her words, the little man held very still. When he turned back to Lily, his dark eyes lightened by degrees, an inner ring of illumination circling his pupils. He blinked rapidly several times.

Lily pressed her advantage. "You are the God of Oaths. You ensure others keep their oaths. Now keep your oath to me. On the sun, you promised the return of my sister for your hound, Failinis."

"Arrggghhhh!" He spun around in fury. He yelled at the ceiling while his body kept spinning in the spot he stood. A golden light sheathed his body. "Stop!"

Thunder cracked in the room. Failinis leapt to his feet and howled.

Lugh's spin increased in speed until he was a blur. Lily covered her ears, and Rose did the same. A howling wind whipped inside the cave. The wind tore at Lily's eyes. Hair slashed across her forehead, cheeks, and neck.

The leprechaun yelled into the storm, a guttural sound, like an animal.

Then Lily screamed into the wind. "God of Oaths, show yourself."

Light filled the interior so bright that even behind closed eyes, Lily's vision turned white. She fell to the ground, covering her head.

Not more blinding light!

Then everything quieted. The wind dissipated.

Gingerly, Lily raised her head to peer around the cavern.

Lugh the leprechaun was gone.

A tall, handsome warrior with radiant blond hair and gleaming armor stood in his place. The man was more beautiful than any one person Lily had ever seen. More beautiful than even Hera.

She gained her feet, brushing off dirt and sand that stuck to her from the whirlwind.

The man, the god, who faced her looked lost. He stared down at his hands, which trembled.

"Lugh?" she asked.

His golden eyelashes swept up, revealing eyes so light in color they were neither blue nor gray, but sadness swam in their depths. Suddenly, he whipped around. He rushed to Rose, who was still on her hands and knees.

She coughed a few times, and he helped her to her feet. His hand gently brushed hair off her cheeks. The movement and the look on his face reflected true care for her, although she looked confused.

Lily's mouth gaped open. Failinis nudged her hand for a reassuring pat.

When Lugh spoke, his voice was deep and tender. "Are you unhurt, Mousie?"

Rose tilted her chin to look up at him, her cheeks pinkening at his concentrated stare. "I'm not hurt."

He smiled but his lips trembled. His eyes gleamed with wetness. "My son, Mousie."

Rose stroked his forearm. "I know."

Then they shared an embrace. Lugh sighed, and the room turned brighter. He clicked his fingers and the chains fell away from her ankle. An echo of other chains releasing and hitting the rocky floor resounded from deeper in the cave.

The minute her sister was free, and Lily understood that she had beaten the leprechaun, she rushed to Rose. They shared a hug tighter than either one of them had ever shared before between them. An overwhelming sensation burst from Lily's chest, rising to her throat and stinging as tears. "I thought I had lost you."

As she said the words, a flash of images coursed through her mind's eye. She anticipated a land animal would be the one trying to communicate with her, but the images were laced with such powerful emotions that she was glad to be holding onto her sister or she might have fallen back.

She saw a wolf sniffing along the ground. The smell of blood created a frenzy in her. Then the wolf shape-shifted into a crow that flew above treetops until coming to a plain. The red field was littered with fighting men and the dead and the dying. She, the crow, screeched her joy at the sight.

Then the images faded.

Lily blinked several times and backed away from Rose, who peered at her with concern.

"Lil?"

Before Lily could answer, Cúig bounded through the cave and knocked into her. She laughed aloud and threw arms around his shaggy neck, inhaling his musky scent, a scent that had become so familiar to her. She was so happy he was alive that tears brimmed in her eyes. She dashed them away, only to find Fintan before her.

Somehow, he looked older than before as he leaned wearily on his walking staff. "It's good to see you, girl." He raised bushy eyebrows at Lugh, who was back at Rose's side, a hand on the side of her face as he spoke softly to her.

Lily couldn't hear the words but was curious about them. Fintan's voice drew her attention back.

"I see you accomplished what I couldn't."

"Rose gave me the clue I needed. She knew what to do to push him to confront what he was hiding from himself." Lily nibbled her lip for a moment. Then she threw her arms around Fintan, and the old man startled. "I couldn't have come to *Tír fo Thuinn* the first time without you. Thank you."

Fintan patted her on the back, nodding as if that seemed right to him, then he sniffed back tears as he pulled away from the hug. "I'm glad I could be there when you needed someone." Then he shuffled around to face the newly formed god. "Well, my boy, I guess your sister will be satisfied that you are not hiding anymore. She feared mightily for you and for others who gained your wrath."

Lugh stepped toward the old man, placing a hand on his shoulder. "I am sorry for my treatment of you." With his free hand, he waved in the air, and it shimmered in the familiar portal to another realm. "Go be with Ébliu. Tell my sister not to worry any longer. I will come visit soon."

Fintan smiled. With one last look at Lily, giving her a wink, he went through the portal which blinked with a brief, bright light before it shrunk away when he stepped through.

"Now," Lugh said, "I must right one more thing."

He looked at Cúig the bear and clapped his hands. Bright light flashed again, and the bear disappeared. In his place stood the Greek soldier, Quintus. The very same man Lily had felt so responsible for losing in the beginning of her journeys.

For the briefest of moments, he stood before them naked, but Lugh waved his hands, and clothes appeared on the Greek man.

Immediately, Lily felt drawn to him, her feet moving on their own toward him, the feeling partly familiar from the time she had spent with him in his bear form. However, part of the familiarity seemed foreign to her, as if she had known him before.

She reached out a hesitant hand, which he quickly met by lacing his fingers with hers. His musky scent surrounded her. Another image crashed through her mind, and she closed her eyes. Another vision.

She saw herself, but with a different face. She clung to a tall man, tears in her eyes. A battle raged all around. The man kissed her, then walked into the battle, leaving his life with her behind.

Lily cried out. "You've been gone so long."

The image left her, and she opened her eyes.

Quintus smiled. "Hallo there."

Still confused and reeling from all the visions, she shook her head. She licked her dry lips. Her legs felt weak. "What happened to you?"

Quintus rubbed the middle of his forehead, closing his eyes momentarily. "When I got separated from you, I decided to find the leprechaun's gold. I thought that since I had exhausted my own wealth, stealing more might help me find my brother." He kept a firm grip on Lily's hand as he faced Lugh. "Of course, chasing a leprechaun and his gold is folly. When Lugh found me searching for him, he changed me into the bear."

Lugh folded his hands over his heart. "Please forgive me, my friend. A natural consequence of being a leprechaun is no care for anyone or their motivations."

Quintus laughed nervously. "Believe me, I know now. But here I am, human again, and I still haven't found my brother." He looked at Lily. "Perhaps you would consider still helping me?"

Lily's first instinct was to say yes. A large part of her being knew that she needed to be with Quintus, but then she remembered that meant picking up their previous plans to visit Mug Ruith, the *Ard-Draoi*. Somehow, she didn't think the man would welcome her back in his home.

Rose cleared her throat. All eyes turned to her, and she held out her arm. The eagle hopped into a short flight to reach her and perched upon her limb. She gazed fondly at the eagle. "Your brother is here."

"What she says is the truth," Lugh said.

Lily furrowed her brow. "You turned him, too?"

The god shook his head. "I cannot claim that transformation."

Rose stroked the eagle's chest. "It was a woman. From what I can put together. He started a love affair with a beautiful but married woman. When he tried to break it off by telling her husband, she turned him into this. But he flew away. He's been running ever since."

"Hera!" Quintus voiced the name as almost a whisper, then spoke more loudly. "Agathon told me that he was having an affair with Hera, and I just assumed she was some wealthy woman. But if the woman had the power to change him..."

Lily's mind had followed a similar track as Quintus's. Hera had asked her to bring her pet eagle back to her. "Then his affair was with the goddess Hera."

The Greek shook his head as he looked to the ground. "I have my faith, but I wouldn't have believed Hera would have an affair with a mortal. The stories suggest some gods do, but I never thought it possible of the goddess."

Lily took a deep breath to deliver the bad news. "She still looks for him." Then she told them how she came back into the Otherworld.

Quintus looked worried. "I don't want the goddess tracking you down next and hurting you, but we cannot hand my brother over."

"I will stay with the girls and protect them," Lugh said.

The statement surprised Lily, but then she saw the look the god gave her sister. *Was it possible that he was in love with Rose?* That could explain why Rose was able to reach him in his leprechaun state.

"But how do I help my brother?" Quintus directed his question to Lugh. "Can you change him back?"

Lugh approached the eagle, who flew to his outstretched arm. He concentrated on the bird as if trying to see deep inside him, then shook his head. "This is a foreign magic. I cannot undo it. Perhaps only Hera can, or any of the Greek gods may be able to help." He looked at Quintus. "You'd be better going to Zeus himself."

Quintus's dark skin lightened by several degrees. "I wouldn't even know how to find him."

"Mount Olympus?" Lugh asked with a short laugh.

Quintus nodded, but the color had not returned to his face. "I know the place, but mortals are not allowed to approach."

Lugh shook his arm, dislodging the eagle, then he turned on his heel to go deeper in his cave. Lily exchanged quizzical glances with the others at hearing an awful raucous echo back to them. The eagle hopped along the ground, chirping. Then the god returned.

He carried two items. The first was a piece of cloth and the other a drinking goblet made of gold and embellished with gems that gleamed in the firelight. He handed both to the Greek. "The magical cloth will grow into a cloak when you pull it over your head and will make you invisible. This should allow you to enter Mount Olympus. It hides others even from the most powerful. Then, the Goblet of Truth. Offer this to Zeus in exchange for help with your brother."

The Greek's mouth dropped open, then realized it and took a deep breath. "What would I have to give you in exchange?"

Lugh shook his head. "This is recompense for your time as a bear and the grief I have brought you." He tapped the goblet in Quintus's hand. "Tell him how this works. If someone speaks three lies over it, it will break into three pieces. But if that same person then speaks the truth, the goblet will be made whole again."

Quintus took a deep breath. "Your plan may work." As he looked over the items in his hands, he slowly nodded, then smiled. "I will do it."

Using one hand, Lugh waved in the air yet again, opening another portal. "I cannot get you to Mount Olympus or even anywhere close, because these places are not in my domain. However, I can see you to your home on Crete, since it is connected to both you and your brother."

Quintus dipped his head with tight lips, then faced Lily directly, shifting the objects to one arm. He laid his free hand on the side of her jaw, drawing her face up.

Lily's eyes widened in that split second when she realized what he planned to do, but she let him.

When his lips touched hers, a charge leapt between them, drawing them closer together like lodestones. Images flooded her mind. They were new and inspiring, but she tucked them away for later musings. Instead, she reveled in the warmth that spread from her middle and flooded her body.

She felt a longing she had never felt in this lifetime. She leaned into his hard chest and opened her lips to him. He deepened the kiss.

For that one happy moment, a feeling she had not experienced in so long, Lily felt at peace at long last. She'd never forget losing her sister, Marigold, but the promise of a new future awaited her.

When Quintus pulled away, loss shook her body.

He didn't move far from her, only inches from her face. His dark-brown eyes with their golden flecks stared deep into hers. "I will come back for you. I swear by my gods and yours that when I have helped my brother, I will find you. I don't know how I know, but we belong together."

Lily could only nod, not because she wished to be mute again, but because of the loss of his touch, knowing that he would be gone from her life in a matter of moments, and realizing the depth of her own feelings for him, made it hard for her to form words.

He reached up with his hand again, a thumb caressing her cheek. He pressed his lips quickly to hers one last time before spinning around toward the portal, his back stiff. He held out an arm. "Agathon." The eagle flew to him, hanging on as Quintus stepped through the portal without looking back.

Lily swallowed hard against the quick flash of light. How could all these feelings come crashing on her now when she should have been happier than she had been in a long time? She finally had her sister back.

Rose raced to her and threw her arms around her. "I'm so glad you found Quintus. I know he'll be back for you."

Lily felt stiff in her sister's arms, still stunned by her own feelings for the Greek and his quick departure.

"And I'm so glad you came back for me."

That loosened Lily, reminding her that Rose was finally free. She hugged her sister hard. "I would do whatever I could to save you. I only wish I could have saved Marigold."

"I know." Rose pulled back, her hands linked with Lily's. Tears shone in her eyes. "You would have done the same for Marigold. But there's nothing else you can do, so stop blaming yourself." A sudden smile lit her face. "I want to know how you traveled back to *Tir fo Thuinn*. It had to be magic..."

Lily smiled, nodding at the same time. "Yes, it was magic. Do you remember when we had all those Greek visitors on the first day of Samhain—"

Lugh's grunt interrupted her.

In unison, with wide eyes, Lily and Rose looked at him.

Failinis woofed.

The god raised a golden eyebrow. "Are you ready to leave?"

They nodded at the same time, then dissolved in giggles.

When Lugh raised a hand for the last time, a portal wider than any of the ones he'd created before shimmered in welcome.

Rose linked her arm through Lily's.

"Let's go home."

Together, they walked through the portal into the blinding light.

CHAPTER 30

LILY PUSHED ASIDE a few bush branches to see if she could spy the lavender-flowered Lus na *gCnámh mBriste*, literally known as the plant for broken bones. It really had multiple uses: cuts, burns, upset stomach, bleeding gums, as well as for use in a poultice. Now that Ana—the Morrígan—was no longer a part of the household, they all had to find remedies for the occasional sickness, scrapes, and broken bones. The delicate flower and its roots were the perfect herb for their stores.

Thank the Mother Goddess that the chill of winter had passed, taking with it the daily reminder that Lily could have somehow prevented Marigold's death. Not that Lily didn't think of her other sister anymore, only that she rarely cried from guilt now. The tears came because she still missed her. Instead, she remembered the best parts of her sister and cherished those memories.

Spring brought warm winds and happier days. Every morning, the sun revealed a forest coming awake with more emerald colors and trees thickened with new leaves. Flowers bloomed. Herbal medicines needed to be stocked, so Lily dug in the ground where she found the purple flower. A few paces from her, Rose also looked for the same herb in a damp section of the forest. They needed a stockpile before the end of the year. No telling if a new druidic healer would come their way.

Lily picked up a clod of wet grass and dirt, balling it in her hands, then slung it toward her sister. Rose screeched as it plopped on her hand, spattering mud everywhere. Failinis barked happily, his tail wagging as if he wanted to get in on the fun. He distracted Lily with several sloppy kisses. Rose returned her own shot but missed. Lily stuck out her tongue. "I'm the warrior in this family," she said, her tone teasing.

Hand over heart and looking skyward, Rose replied, "Thank the gods that makes me the smart one."

Lily chuckled, then sobered. Rose really was more intelligent than Lily had given her credit for. Always seeing her sister as the naïve one, too trusting, too impulsive.

But Rose had not only persevered in being a prisoner, but she had also devised and worked on a plan to turn her captor. Now Lugh wouldn't leave her side unless Ciara required work of him. Unfortunately for him, he was one of the few males capable of the more demanding tasks at the *ráth*.

That reminded Lily of something that she had forgotten for all these months. "What did Lugh say to you when he first changed from being the leprechaun?"

Pink flushed across Rose's cheeks, and she turned her attention back to digging out the flower by the root. "He said that he was in love with me and that he wouldn't leave me until I either returned his feelings or fell in love with another."

Lily sat back on her heels, thoughtful. "Could you love him or ever be in love with him?"

Rose brushed a red curl from her face, leaving a smudge of mud on her cheek. She shrugged. "He's a gorgeous man, and I think the Lugh we know now is a good person. But love him?" She sneezed, then stared at the ground, followed by the hardening of her mouth corners. "I cannot forget that he held me captive." She held up her fisted hands, and they shook. Her blue eyes flashed with anger as she met Lily's stare. Then her whole face softened. "But can I hold that against him? I don't know." Her voice trailed off as she lowered her hands to her lap. "Besides, how would I know if I was in love with him?"

Lily knew.

Her heart still flipped against her chest whenever she thought of Quintus, and the vision she had had of them.

She dug her hands back into the warm earth. Rose chattered on, steering the conversation away from her feelings about Lugh. She told one story Lily had heard a dozen times before, so she hummed quietly under her breath, her mind wandering.

Suddenly Rose's voice trailed off, pausing.

"Do you hear that?" she asked.

Lily held still, straining her ears, and sent out a questing to the animals in the area. A small group of deer, does with their new fawns, had stuck around when Lily had reassured them that she and Rose had planned to leave them alone.

They relayed images of rustling to the south. Probably no more than a couple dozen paces away. Failinis looked in the same direction.

She rose to her feet, shrugging on her satchel filled with the needed herb. Her sister followed, letting her guide them as she had a better connection with the animals on the ground. As they neared the source of the sound, they could make out a male voice cursing at the forest.

Then they finally came upon the man. Both stopped in surprise, staying out of sight. Lily held a hand out to Failinis, communicating for him to fall back. Lily and Rose hid in the shadows of several tightly packed evergreens.

The man in front of them couldn't be much more than two feet tall. He was caught in a blackthorn shrub. The sharp points of the plant poked through his gold-embroidered, red jacket, his black trousers, and his long, white beard.

Lugh?

No, he was back home, digging holes for new posts for the defense of *Ráth Bláthanna*. Besides, he hadn't taken the form of the leprechaun since he had changed back.

This must be a new and different leprechaun caught in the middle of their forest. *What were the odds of it happening again?*

Lily exchanged a glance with Rose. They both shook their heads and started to retreat, Failinis following.

"I hear you, you scum! Come help me!"

Lily covered her mouth to stop a laugh, but neither of them stayed around long enough to hear the rest of the leprechaun's curses.

When Lily finally spotted the worn path back to their home *ráth*, the little man's voice was too distant to be heard clearly. She breathed a sigh of relief, looking behind her as Rose came up on the path from the tree line. Failinis danced between them, his eyes sparkling.

Rose gave her a wide smile, her blue eyes lighting in mirth. "Not doing that again!"

No. They wouldn't be caught in the folly of a leprechaun again. Lily could have hugged her sister right then, but something itched in the middle of her back. Some sort of intuition breaking through to her awareness.

A slight wind shifted through the air, bringing the scent of the sun passing through new leaves, with a hint of coriander and the rough scent of bark.

Then she smelled a familiar scent. Rowanberries hung on every tree, their aromas bursting through the air, but it was the underlying musk that touched her memories. She whipped around on the path.

Just ahead of her about twenty paces away, Quintus stood. Her heart stopped, and she lifted her hand to her chest. All the times she wondered whether she had only imagined that she'd loved the Greek now flew away.

She knew she loved this man.

She took one light, bouncing step toward him. Then stopped.

Agathon the eagle perched on his shoulder.

She winced with a heavy sigh. The eagle meant their quest had failed. Quintus's stony face confirmed her suspicion. Dread dropped a heavy iron pit into her stomach.

"We need your help."

DID YOU ENJOY THE NOVEL?

If you loved this story, it would mean a lot to me if you leave a review on Amazon, Goodreads, BookBub, or any other social media platform of your choice. Even just a line or two would be incredibly helpful.

This story continues with Rose as the main character with a few other points of view sprinkled in like the Morrígan. Would you like to read the first three chapters of *Soul of Rose* right now? Sign up for my author newsletter at https://bit.ly/sdhuston-newsletter.

ACKNOWLEDGMENTS

Thank you to my husband and sons for being supportive and understanding of my life as a writer.

Thank you to Nissa Leder for reading all my words and not only offering insight to improve my writing, but also for urging me for the last five years to finally publish!

Last, thank you to all of my beta readers and critique partners. Your care and insight have helped to make this the best story possible!

GLOSSARY

No fixed rule has been followed as to the spelling and pronunciation of Irish names and places. Various good authorities and sources publish Irish names with differing spellings, so complete accuracy is not possible. Additionally, names vary in pronunciation by region and dialect, not withstanding the fact that several Irish sounds do not have an English counterpart. The suggested pronunciations below are those that I used in my head when drafting the story based on the best evidence found while researching for this novel.

Pronunciation Guide

Pronunciation of vowels:

a short, like *man*
e short, like *err*
i short, like *ill*
o short, like *other*
u short, like *up*

á long, like *awe*
é long, like *there*
í long, like *eel*
ó long, like *old*
ú long, like *rule*

Agathon—a Greek man; Quintus's missing brother

Alannah (Ah-lon-a)—aunt to Lily and her sisters; sister to Ciara

An Abhainn As Ceann Mhara (Ah-na-ouw-enn ah-s kown m-wa-ra)—The River at the Head of the Sea

An Abhainn Bradán (Ah-na-ouw-enn Bruh-don)—The Salmon River, a river close to *Ráth Bláthanna*

An Caladh (Ah-n Ca-wall)—The Rest Place by the Sea, a settlement close to *Oileán Dairbhre*

An Caorthann Coill (Ah-n Queer-un Qu-will)—The Rowan Woods, a forest around *Ráth Bláthanna*

Ana (A-na)—a *bandraoi*, a female druid, Ciara's lover for sixteen years and second mother to her children

Ard-Draoi (Awe-rd-dwree)—High Druid; name given to Mug Ruith

Ardgal (ARD-ul)—Warrior of Valor in *Tír fo Thuinn*

Balor (Baa-lowr)—a leader of the Fomorians; often described as a giant with a large eye that wreaks destruction when opened; takes part in the Battle of Magh Tuireadh, and is primarily known from the tale in which he is killed by his grandson Lugh of the Tuatha Dé Danann

bandraoi (Ban-dwree)—female druid

Battle of Magh Tuireadh (Mawg Tur-rid)—also known as Cath Magh Tuireadh; the name of two saga texts of the Mythological Cycle of Irish mythology; refers to two separate battles in Connacht; the two texts tell of battles fought by the Tuatha Dé Danann, the first against the Fir Bolg, and the second against the Fomorians

Bealach Béime (Bay-lach bey-am)—Pass of the Notch; one of Ireland's wildest passes, extremely steep on both sides, with barely any level ground; cuts through the mountains where the steep slopes of Mullagahanattin to the south and Knockaunattin to the north form a distinctive "V"

Bealach Oisín (Bay-lach Oh-sheen)—Oisín's Pass; pass connects Glencar and the interior of the Iveragh Peninsula with the Inny Valley, which leads down to the coast at Waterville

cailleach (KAL-yach)—a divine hag and ancestor, associated with the creation of the landscape and with the weather, especially storms and winter; an expression of the hag or crone archetype found throughout world cultures

Cha d'dhùin doras nach d'fhosgail doras (Caw dih-doo-inn durriss nock dus-gall duriss)—a saying that roughly translates to: "No door closed without another opening."

Ciara (Ka-ra or KEE-ir-a)—mother to Lily, Rose, and Marigold; lover of Ana; lives at *Ráth Bláthanna*

Clann Séaghdha (Clown Shay)—the clan Lily and her family belong to

Cloch na Coille (Clo-gh nah Qu-will)—the Woodstone fortress; the fortress belonging to the *Ard-Draoi*, the High Druid Mug Ruith

Coilean mac Domangairt (Qu-lawn mac Doe-min-girt)—second oldest son to Domangart; lives at *Ráth Bláthanna*

Cúchulainn (Coo-haul-inn)—an Irish mythological demigod who appears in the stories of the Ulster Cycle

Cúig (Ku-wig)—means five; name given to Lily's animal companion

Dagda, the (DAHG-duh)—a member of the Tuatha Dé Danann; portrayed as a father-figure, king, and druid; associated with fertility, agriculture, manliness and strength, as well as magic, druidry and wisdom; can control life and death, the weather and crops, as well as time and the seasons; "the good god" or "the great god"; other names include Eochu or Eochaid Ollathair ("horseman, great father" or "all-father")

Dáire (DAW-reh)—a soldier following the Warrior of Valor in *Tír fo Thuinn*

Danu (Da-noo)—mother goddess of the Tuatha Dé Danann

Dermot (Der-mutt)—one of the only available males not related by blood who is ordered by his *taoiseach* to marry either Lily or Rose; shares a passion of harp-playing with Lily; chooses Lily as his partner

Domangart—steward of *Ráth Bláthanna*; father to Odhran, Coilean, Blathnaid, one other unnamed son, and Sorcha, a daughter who died several years ago; lame-footed

draoi (Dwree)—male druid

dún (Doo)—an ancient or medieval fortress; mainly a kind of hillfort; a term usually used for any stronghold of importance, which may or may not be ring-shaped

Dún Neidín (Doo Ne-gene)—home to the *taoiseach* (clan chief) of *Clann Séaghdha*

Éire (Ire)—one of the ancient names given to Ireland

Enbarr (An-baa)—a horse in the Irish Mythological Cycle which could traverse both land and sea, and was swifter than wind-speed; property of the sea God Manannán mac Lir, but provided to Lugh to use at his disposal

Failbhe mac Diarmuid Mór (Fal-vhe mac Deer-m-wood Moor)— grandson of *Clann Séaghdha*'s *taoiseach*, Rindal an Carragh, and cousin to Lily and Rose

Failinis (Faw ihn-ish)—hound belonging to Lugh

Fintan mac Bóchra (FIN-tan mac BOW-chra)—known as "the Wise"; a seer who accompanied Noah's granddaughter Cessair to Ireland before the deluge; his sixteen wives and children drowned when the flood arrived, but he survived in the form of a salmon; survived into the time of Fionn mac Cumhaill, becoming the repository of all knowledge of Ireland and all history

Fionn mac Cumhaill (Fyun mac coo-al)—a mythical hunter-warrior in Irish mythology; stories of Fionn and his followers, the Fianna, form the Fenian Cycle; father to Oisín

Flidais (Flih-ddish)—goddess of the hunt, wild animals, and the forest

Jason—hound belonging to Hera

Hera—Greek woman who visits *Ráth Bláthanna*

Lily—also known as Líle níc Muaich (Lee-luh nick ?) and Sneachta Bán (Sh-nack-da Baa-n) or Snow White; sister to Rose and Marigold; blames herself for Marigold's death; lives at *Ráth Bláthanna*

Lir (Leer)—a member of the Tuatha Dé Danann; god of the sea; chiefly an ancestor figure, and is the father of the god Manannán mac Lir; appears as the eponymous king in the tale *The Children of Lir*

Lugh (Loo)—a grumpy and ungrateful leprechaun

Máel Maud (Maw Mauwd)—*Dún Neidín*'s head warrior

mamaí (Maw-mee)—mother

Manannán mac Lir (Mana-non mac leer)—a member of the Tuatha Dé Danann; a warrior and king of the Otherworld; associated with the sea and often interpreted as a sea god; son of Lir

Mórrígan / the Morrígan (Moh-ree-*gh*an)—a member of the Tuatha Dé Danann; goddess of war, death, and prophecy

Mug Ruith (Moi Rwee)—the *Ard-Draoi*, the High Druid; the most powerful Druid in Èire

Na Cailíní Bláth (Nuh Ky-lee-nee Blow)—the flower girls, the nickname given to Lily, Rose, and Marigold when Marigold had been alive

Niamh Chinn Óir (Nee-av Keen Oiluh)—a member of the Tuatha Dé Danann, daughter of Manannán mac Lir; took Oisín, son of Fionn mac Cumhaill, to *Tír na nÓg*; mother to Oscar, Fionn, and Plor

Odhran mac Domangairt (UR-awn mac Doe-min-girt)—oldest son to Domangart; lives at *Ráth Bláthanna*

Oileán Dairbhre (Eh-lawn Der-vrah)—the Isle of Oaks, home to the *Ard-Draoi*, the High Druid Mug Ruith

Oisín (Oh-sheen)—son of Fionn mac Cumhaill; a warrior of the Fianna; marries Niamh Chinn Óir and lives with her in *Tír na nÓg*; father to Oscar, Fionn, and Plor with Niamh

Paiste (Posh-teh)—also known as Lig na Paiste (Lehg no Posh-teh); a giant serpent; he could spit fire and venom in equal measure, tall as two men standing one atop the other at the shoulder, with mighty curling ram's horns; an ancient remnant from the beginning of the world; the last dragon of Ireland

Quintus—a Greek warrior who comes to Éire searching for his brother Agathon

ráth (Ra)—a circular fortified settlement

Ráth Bláthanna (Ra Blow-hun-ah)—home to Lily and her family

Rindal an Carragh (Ree-n-dahl ah-n car-rah)—Rindal the Scabby; *taoiseach*, the chief of *Clann Séaghdha*, leader of numerous settlements including *Ráth Bláthanna*

Rose—also known as Rós níc Muaich (Rose nick ?) and Rós Dearg (Rose Darr-ig) or Rose Red; sister to Lily and Marigold; lives at *Ráth Bláthanna*

Samhain (Sow-when)—a Gaelic festival marking the end of the harvest season and beginning of winter or "darker-half" of the year

taoiseach (TEE-shock)—clan chief; chieftain or leader

tíolacadh (Dye-la-ka-th)—a gift of magical powers

Tír fo Thuinn (Tear foe-hen)—"Land Under the Waves," part of the Celtic Otherworld

Tír na nÓg (Tear na naw-g)—"Land of Youth," part of the Celtic Otherworld; best known from the tale of Oisín and Niamh

Tuatha Dé Danann (Too-a-ha day Donnan)—"the folk of the goddess Danu," a supernatural race in Irish mythology

ABOUT THE AUTHOR

Told that she was a weird child because she spent summers in the backrooms of libraries reading and drawing everything she researched, S.D. Huston embraced her eccentric passions for writing. Even as she constantly traveled all her life with some years spent in the U.S. Army, then gaining an MFA in creative writing from Spalding University, she always immersed herself in reading and writing about magical lands and world mythologies. She particularly loves Irish mythology with its Celtic roots, which found its way center stage in her YA Fantasy novel, *Blood of the Lily*. She continues to embrace all the quirkiness in her life, especially her autistic son who sees life as one grand adventure filled with beasts and monsters that need to be conquered. Other love interests include her family, four cats, and one dog.

CONNECT WITH S.D. HUSTON ON:

Website: www.sdhuston.com
YouTube: www.youtube.com/channel/UCBY1ZdiOkr2qBrn0y7aOhBw
Facebook: www.facebook.com/SDHuston.Author
Twitter: twitter.com/SD_Huston
Instagram: instagram.com/s.d.huston

Made in the USA
Coppell, TX
26 October 2021